Other Books

MW00949434
WITHDRAWN

Fiction

<u>THE LOST CITY CHRONICLES</u>

Legend of the Book Keeper

City of Gold

Earthly Trinity

Return to a Lost City (novella)

<u>THE GALLOWOOD FILES</u>

Case #1: *The Painter's Portal*

<u>CHILDREN'S BOOKS</u>

Two Thankful Turtles

Non-Fiction

When Worlds Collide: Stepping Up and Standing Out in an Anti-God Culture

7 Steps to Knowing, Doing, and Experiencing the Will of God for Teens

WITHDRAWN

Siloam Springs Public Library
205 East Jefferson Street
Siloam Springs, AR 72761

Copyright © 2017 by Daniel R. Blackaby

All rights reserved. This book or any portion thereof may not be reproduced or used in any manner whatsoever without the express written permission of the publisher except for the use of brief quotations in a book review.

First Printing, September 2017

Printed in the United States of America

Interior Illustrations by Morgan Davis

Cover Design by Sarah Emily Blackaby

ISBN-13: 978-1548649692

ISBN-10: 1548649694

BISAC: Fiction / Thrillers / Supernatural

Black-A-Bee Creations Publishing

305 Cobb Court

Hampton, GA 30228

www.danielblackaby.com

To Mike and Carrie.

...for a childhood full of crazy memories and book material.

Sometimes truth really is stranger than fiction.

THE GALLOWOOD FILES

Case #1

"The Painter's Portal"

Written by Daniel Blackaby

Illustrations by Morgan Davis

The following is a true account based upon my meticulous investigations into recent peculiar events in the small town of Gallowood (not real name). This narrative has been pieced together through firsthand testimonials (names have been changed due to the still ongoing nature of my investigation). I have, to the best of my ability and knowledge, not exaggerated or omitted any relevant details. I will also note that, in order to maintain authenticity, I have written in the casual vernacular of the subjects. A more scholarly account will be written at a later date. By choosing to publish these previously classified case files, I hope to enlist your aid in helping to solve the troubling, supernatural mysteries occurring in Gallowood. So please read on and discover the incident that initially drew my attention – the bizarre case of The Painter's Portal.

– Dr. Daniel R. Blackaby, Private Inspector

The House At the End of Hallow's Drive

The house at the end of Hallow's Drive was haunted. Every kid in Gallowood knew so. While their parents would obviously never affirm such silly superstitions, they had the curious habit of taking the *long way* through town, somehow managing to avoid ever coming within four or five blocks of

the lonely mansion. They claimed it was merely coincidence, but their kids knew the truth (and not one raised so much as a peep in complaint).

No other homes occupied Hallow's Drive. This had not *always* been the case. If pressed hard enough, some of the older children on the playground would confess that there had once been *dozens* of other houses—normal homes with normal families. Then one fateful morning the people of Gallowood awoke only to find that the other houses had vanished without a trace! When asked what became of the missing homes and happy families, the storyteller would refuse to speak any more on the topic, and would only whisper the same solemn warning: *Never, under any circumstances, go near that haunted house at the end of Hallow's Drive.*

Now, some of you older and more skeptical readers might think this is an exaggeration. You might even be tempted to dismiss it all as a silly story intended to terrify young children. If so, that is only because you have, thus far, had the tremendous fortune of staying far away from the house at the end of Hallow's Drive. For the unlucky few who have found themselves standing in the shade of its sinister shadow, however, these tales are no laughing matter. Such is the fateful account of the three Cavanaugh children. Their story begins, like many terrifying tales, beneath the full-moon of a chilly October night....

"I don't *care* if it's a short-cut," Catherine said, yanking on her frizzled, blonde ponytail and following several paces behind her two older brothers.

"Mom warned us not to be late," James said, in a patronizing tone. "This is the quickest way." At fourteen years old he was the eldest and therefore the undisputed authority of their pack.

"I don't care. *I don't want to be here.*"

Right on cue, a gust of wind billowed down the street like the wailing moans of an angry ghoul, and the temperature dipped by several degrees.

"*Please,*" Catherine pleaded.

"You're such a scaredy-cat." The taunt came, as always, from Ricky.

"Am not!"

"Are too." Ricky grabbed his cheeks and chattered his teeth. "I'm Catherine, and I want my mommy!" He stuck a thumb into his mouth and sucked on it like a baby.

"Stop it! James, make him stop!" Before James could intervene, another bluster of wind blew over them. Ricky's face went white. He lifted a shaky finger and pointed behind her. "It's...it's...*A GHOST*!"

Catherine shrieked, leapt three feet into the air, and launched her armful of school papers into the wind. She spun—and saw nothing but empty street.

Ricky cackled. "*Told you* you're a scaredy-cat!" Catherine punched his shoulder.

"Cut it out, you two," James said, acting as peacekeeper between his bickering siblings. "Hurry and help Catherine gather her stuff. We need to get home. Mom will be worried." His quivering voice suggested there was another, *more urgent*, reason he wanted to get going.

Ricky and Catherine knelt to retrieve the papers, continuing their quarrel in whispers too soft for James to hear. As Catherine reached for the final sheet, it leapt off the ground and flitted away like a leaf on the breeze. She lunged, but the page danced away just beyond her nine-year-old reach. She gritted her teeth and scampered down the street after it.

A menacing shadow fell over her. Catherine skidded to a stop. An arched gate now stood before her. Leafy vines clung to the weather-beaten stone like plump leeches and two gargoyles flanked the gate, their marble eyeballs peering directly at her. Catherine stared through the gate at a building thirty feet away—the house at the end of Hallow's Drive.

Her breath jammed in her throat as she retreated back to the street. The trio watched as the piece of paper pirouetted across the weed-infested lawn and was caught by the claw-like branches of the dead, rotting hedges below the mansion's window. Dusty blinds concealed any view of the haunted carnival inside. The wind rattled the window shades against the wall with a steady *clunk...clunk...clunk.* The noise was joined only by the soft tinkling of wind chimes and the heavy breathing of the three children.

"Let's go," James whispered.

"I *can't,*" Catherine said. "That's the permission slip for tomorrow's field trip."

"Nobody cares about your dumb field trip," Ricky said, already backing away.

Catherine looked at her brother, his shaggy brown hair messy over his widened eyes. "It's the last trip of the year. I'd be the only one not to go! Too bad I'm just a little scaredy-cat." She paused, tapping a finger against her chin. "Good thing I have such a *brave* older brother to retrieve the permission slip for me." Her lips rose into an impish grin. "Unless, of course, *you're* a scaredy-cat, too."

Ricky's face scrunched toward his nose like a folded accordion. He *hated* when the little brat out-maneuvered him! He obviously had no choice now. He puffed out his chest and laughed, intending for it to sound bold and courageous. Instead, it dribbled off his tongue like the squeak of a frightened mouse on helium. He glanced to James for rescue, but his older brother had lowered his eyes, suddenly captivated by a wad of gum stuck to the pavement. Ricky took a deep breath—and stepped forward.

Catherine cried out in alarm, shocked that he would be insane enough to actually do it. With each slow step, Ricky promised God that—if he survived—he'd *never* torment his little sister again. Ever. Or at least until next Tuesday.

The two stone gargoyles greeted him with hostile stares, warning him to turn back. Ricky made a mental list, in alphabetical order, of all the ways Catherine was the worst sister in the history of ever. It was a *long* list.

The manor's front lawn was a jungle, the product of decades of neglect. Weeds and dry grass speared up waist-high, swaying with the wind. As Ricky pushed through the dense foliage, the grass rustled and unseen critters scampered to find refuge elsewhere. Ricky cringed, trying not to think about what was scuttling over his feet. His heart pounded like a hyper child with a drumstick. Neither of his siblings had budged an inch. Their eyes were the size of snow-globes, with Catherine's only partially visible through the fingers shielding her face.

After what seemed like several eternities, Ricky reached the leafless hedge. Catherine's permission slip was entangled deep within the skeletal bush. He reached for it, careful not to cut himself on the dagger-like thorns. His fingertips brushed the paper.

Almost there.

He stretched a little farther.

Behind him, James bellowed. "*RUN!*"

Ricky's head jerked up. Faint light was trickling through the window blinds. He tried to yank his arm free, but his sleeve got snared on the thorns. Desperate, he looked to his siblings for help—but they were already long gone, their footfall fading into the distance.

Ricky was alone.

He tugged again and again but each pull only further entrapped him in branches' death-clasp. A soft noise began to emanate from inside the house.

Creeeeeeeeeeeak...

Creeeeeeeeeeeak...

CREEEEEEEEEEAK....

The window blinds rustled.

Ricky screamed.

He yanked his arm so forcefully that his entire shirt ripped right off his body. The tall grass swallowed him as he fell backwards. Blindly scampering on hands and knees, Ricky emerged from the jungle back into the abandoned street. He risked a final glance back at the cursed house. Peering back at him through the narrow gap between bended blinds were two green, cat-like eyes.

A Warning in Blood

The Cavanaugh children were unusually silent during breakfast. James and Catherine were engaged in an earnest contest to avoid eye-contact at all costs. All the while, Ricky glared at his two despicable siblings with the ferocity of an enraged bull. Yesterday had proven one thing: the house at the end of Hallow's Drive was *not* empty. Goosebumps crawled over Ricky's skin. Those terrible green eyes in the window had been like staring into the depths of two black holes.

The threesome mutely picked at their food for several more minutes until the notoriously impatient James finally forfeited the game of silence. He banged a fist on the table, sending the milk from Catherine's cereal bowl sloshing onto her lap (much to her displeasure). "It was probably our imaginations."

"You don't *have* an imagination," Ricky said. "It was real. I *saw* it. If you hadn't, you know—*abandoned me to die*—you would've seen it, too!"

"Did they get a good look at you?" Catherine asked, voice timid. Ricky nodded. She slapped her cheeks. "*We're all going to die!*"

"No we're not," James said, patting her head reassuringly. "Listen. Even if someone *does* live in that house and even if they *did* see us, it doesn't matter. They never leave that house, right?"

Ricky and Catherine nodded.

"Which means they've never seen us before, right?"

They nodded again.

"That means they don't know who we are. We'll just keep our distance from now on." For perhaps the first time in recorded human history, all three Cavanaugh siblings were in total agreement.

After slurping up the rest of their breakfast, they grabbed their backpacks and headed to the door. Catherine didn't even make a single grumbling remark about missing her field trip. Despite James' reassurance, the foreboding tension in the air was like a giant python wrapping around and slowly crushing the life out of them. "It's going to be okay, guys," James said again. "Trust me." He opened the door.

Laying on the doorstep was a tattered red shirt. It looked almost *identical* to the blue shirt Ricky had lost in the hedges last night. He knelt to retrieve it—and yelped. It *was* his shirt. Only now it was completely soaked in fresh blood.

Child-Eating Monsters and Psychotic Mass Murderers

There was no mistaking the message sent by the bloody shirt:

I KNOW WHERE YOU LIVE.

I KNOW WHAT YOU'VE DONE.

I'M NOT HAPPY ABOUT IT.

Ricky backed away from the door. "What are we going to do?" The youngest two siblings turned to their older brother for guidance. James looked as though his body couldn't decide whether to throw up, faint, or do both at the same time.

"We could run and hide..."

So much for our fearless leader, Ricky thought.

"We should tell dad" Catherine suggested.

Ricky shook his head. "We can't."

"Why not?"

"Because then we'd have to admit we were trespassing. And worst of all..." he dropped his voice to a whisper, "...he'd tell mom." Good point. Their mother was already sour from last night's tardy arrival. When mom wasn't happy—*nobody* was happy.

"We'll be safe at school," James said. "Let's brainstorm and then decide what to do after class. Agreed?"

"Agreed."

Few things scared James. *Spiders* had always topped that shortlist. But last night the eight-legged demons had finally been dethroned. The house at the end of Hallow's Drive and the raging psychopath within were a whole new level of terrifying. James wondered how many innocent young boys the madman had mangled. A hundred-and-fifty-four? *Surely* no less. The skeletons were likely decaying in the mansion's dreary dungeon.

Five long fingers curled around his shoulder. James squealed and flung his hands into the air. He heard his teacher's concerned voice—and then he fainted.

Ricky struggled to focus on school at the best of times. Knowing a cold-blooded, murderous lunatic might appear at any moment made class downright unbearable. As the teacher droned on, Ricky let his thoughts wander.

His frenzied imagination sketched an assortment of possible bodies to go with the chilling green eyes he had seen. Some incarnations included slimy scales; others a spiked scorpion tail (highly poisonous, of course); while still others had vast bat wings. In *all* manifestations the grotesque creature had horns.

Catherine stared bug-eyed ahead as her teacher marked the blackboard. The sound of scraping chalk was unbearable against her jittery nerves. She clung, white-knuckled, to her desk as if she would immediately float into space the moment she let go.

We're going to die.

We're going to die.

Ricky is going to die first.

And then we're going to die.

They made no eye contact as they walked home. Instead, they scanned left and right until their necks cramped; inspecting every bush for signs of a child-eating monster lurking within.

"Okay," James said, clasping his hands together. "What did you two come up with?"

Ricky's eyelid twitched. "Perhaps we were a little too quick to rule out your original plan of running and hiding."

"My thoughts exactly!" Catherine blurted. "Should we run to Mexico or Canada?"

There was a soft rustle as some shrubbery ahead jiggled. The three siblings jumped into a single, entangled clump. Running would be futile. Especially if the monster had wings (which it surely did).

The bush stopped shaking—and a small squirrel pranced out. The furry rodent tilted its head, staring curiously at the three-headed mass of limbs before scurrying away. James wiggled free from Catherine's death-grasp.

"We can't leave Gallowood," he said. "If a killer lives in that house we need to warn the rest of the town."

"I thought you said we *shouldn't* tell anyone?" Catherine asked.

"I did," James said. "At least not without more evidence."

Ricky squeezed his clammy hands together. "Surely you're not suggesting what I *think* you're suggesting, *are you?*"

"I am."

"Are you crazy!" Ricky paused. "Well, I've always known you were completely nuts, but not *this* bonkers!"

"Think," James said. "Until we know the truth, we'll never get another second of sleep for the rest of our lives." Of course, under current circumstances, their lives weren't likely to last much longer anyways. James forced himself to stand straighter. "Maybe it *was* just our imaginations. Or perhaps David Camp is playing another stupid prank on us. Bottom line, we need evidence and we need a witness who can confirm our story."

Ricky ran a hand through his shaggy hair. "Hmmm. I know just the person. My best friend Emily. She has the imagination of a mud-covered brick."

"Good. We'll sneak out after bedtime. No chickening out. Deal?"

"Deal," Ricky said.

"Deal," Catherine said.

That settled it. When the sun set that night, they would return to the house of a deranged killer and whatever grim fate awaited them there.

Siloam Springs Public Library
205 East Jefferson Street
Siloam Springs, AR 72761

Returning to a Nightmare (and Certain Death)

A wispy fog descended on Gallowood, swallowing the small town. From within the swirling haze came the serpentine hiss of the wind, as if blown by the fog itself. At the end of the somber street, obscured by the phantom-like mist, stood a lone mansion.

Four hooded children gazed at the ancient building, too determined to retreat but too fearful to approach. Eventually, one stepped forward. Emily removed her hood, letting her long brown hair spill out. "Can you *please* explain why instead of snoozing in my warm bed I'm being dragged to the home of a psychotic mass murderer?" She punctuated the question with an embellished eye roll.

Emily was perhaps the only Gallowood kid too foolish *not* to believe that the house at the end of Hallow's Drive was brimming with dark, ghoulish beings. Her mind worked like a calculator. If she couldn't see and touch her own nose she would go to her grave denying she'd ever had one.

"So you can prove that I'm right," Ricky said, for what must have been the twenty-fourth time. "No one will believe *us*. But everyone knows you're far too uptight and simple-minded to make up false stories."

"How sweet of you," Emily said through gritted teeth. With a *humph*, she marched toward the house. Ricky quickly followed, not wanting to be shamed by a girl; James fell into step behind Ricky, not wanting to be shamed by a younger brother; and Catherine claimed the caboose, not wanting to be left alone.

When the foursome stopped again, the stone arch gate was directly before them like a set of gaping jaws ready to devour them. Even in the dancing fog, the penetrating eyes of the two gargoyle sentries seemed pinned directly on them. Ricky quivered. He felt as if the stone guardians could somehow see beneath his skin; as though they were feasting upon his fear. If so, then he was a walking all-you-can-eat buffet.

"Sooo," Emily said, twirling a strand of hair with her finger. "What now?"

Good question, Ricky thought. They hadn't thought this far ahead. In the cozy shelter of their home, the idea to return to the haunted mansion at midnight on a dark, foggy night had seemed like a better idea. Actually, no. Come to think of it, it had seemed like a totally horrible idea then, too.

"We need evidence that someone lives here," James said. "And any sign of..." He didn't finish the sentence. He didn't need to. They all knew the words left on his tongue: *Any sign of the dead, mutilated, fly-covered corpses of trespassing children.*

Catherine motioned to Ricky. "This was *your* idea."

He scowled, but before her could remind her that it was, in fact, *James'* terrible idea, he noticed Emily staring at him. He closed his mouth, rubbed his palms together, and then marched toward the house.

"Ricky!" Emily cried, her earlier confidence having apparently abandoned ship. "If you're just trying to prove how brave you are it's *far* too late for that."

Catherine chuckled. The laugher felt as out of place as the tango music played at their great aunt Sue's funeral. Her giggles faded, giving way to the wailing wind.

Ricky looked back over his shoulder. "But I *would* appreciate some company!"

The others shuffled forward through the gateway and into the weed-infested lawn. "We should check the backyard," Catherine suggested, her hushed voice almost inaudible.

"Good idea. Let's split up," James said, taking charge.

"I'll take Catherine around the left side. Ricky and Emily, you go around the right. We'll meet in the back."

They wished each other luck, all secretly wondering if it was the last time they'd ever see each other. Then, without another word, they departed around the sides of the mansion. If not for the dense fog they might have noticed the two green eyes peering at them through the window.

Watching.

Waiting.

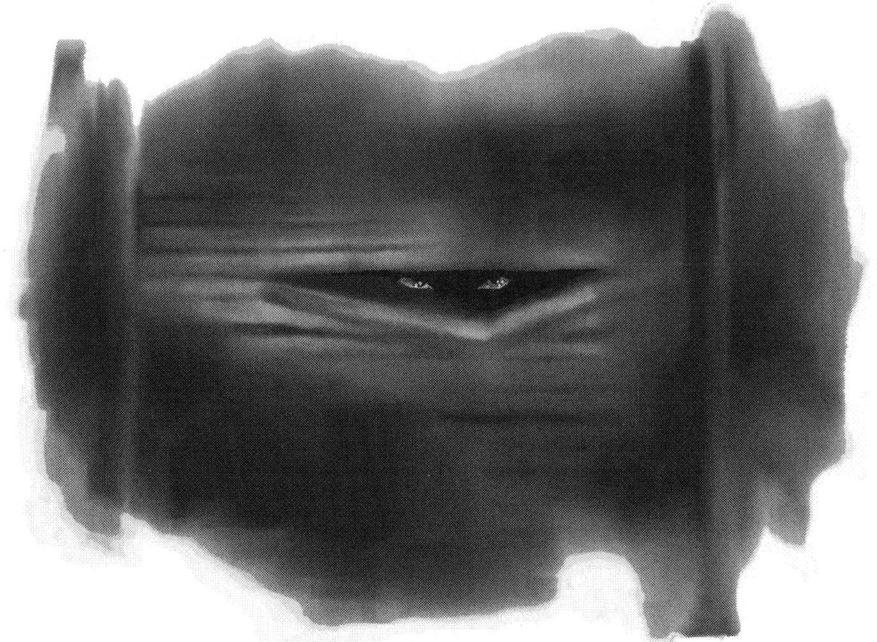

Where the Dead Dwell

Copious spider-webs streamed down from the mansion walls, the silky white nets blanketing the ground and bushes like a thick winter snowfall. All over the webs, a thousand irritated arachnids scurried away as their nests were disturbed by the two intruders...or rather, the *one* intruder.

Catherine turned and placed her hands on her hips. "*Come on,* James. The sooner we finish, the sooner we go home."

James stood several steps back, his face as pale as the spider webs surrounding them. "I can't do it."

Catherine motioned him forward, impatiently. "We're trespassing on a killer's haunted property, and the part that scares you most is *the spiders?*"

"YES!" James looked dumbfounded, as if she had just

asked if the sky would still be blue tomorrow.

Catherine rolled her eyes. "I'll let Ricky and Emily know why you ran home and abandoned your one-and-only baby sister." She pressed on, using a stick to cut through the webs as through she were hacking through jungle foliage with a machete. Moments later she heard an exasperated grunt as James scampered to catch up.

The mansion was huge. The black-shingled roof seemed to spear up halfway to the full moon. Oddly, there were no windows of any sort. Only cracked bricks and spider webs. *Lots and lots* of spider webs. James stepped on Catherine's heels as they inched forward, their chests heaving in unison.

BOOM!

The sky erupted, sending violent tremors through the ground.

Then the rain began to pour.

Hard water pellets bombarded them like an artillery barrage. The sky lit up as a chain of white lightning whipped across the horizon. "Okay, *now* we need to go," James said. This time Catherine voiced no protest. They turned to flee but hesitated. Ricky and Emily would likely assume they'd been captured...or worse. Drenched or not, they had to press on. Catherine pulled her hood down to shield her face from the onslaught. "Quick!"

They ran, abandoning all caution. Spider webs wrapped

around and clung to their faces. They soon had the appearance of two reanimated mummies having escaped their Egyptian crypt. James frantically clawed to remove the sticky webs. He could feel the pattering of a hundred tiny feet marching through his spiked hair. *Could things possibly get any worse?*

Catherine came to an abrupt stop. James, still flailing at the webs, slammed into her back and sent them both tumbling to the ground. Catherine gasped, too winded to speak. Instead she raised her hand and pointed. Apparently things *could* get worse. *Much* worse. Jutting out from the ground, as far as they could see, were row upon row of tombstones.

The First Victim

Ricky and Emily moved forward like two plodding slugs. Whether the result of their glacial pace or merely the immensity of the mansion, their journey to the backyard felt like hours—terrible, traumatic, torturous hours. The lofty building shielded them from the wind, but the result was something far worse—complete silence.

Emily motioned for Ricky to stop. "Do you see that?"

He squinted, peering through the fog. "See what?"

She grabbed his chin and aimed his sightline toward a leafless tree. Its sprawling branches speared toward the moonlit sky like the legs of a giant upturned cockroach. Perched upon one of the skeletal branches was the world's largest vulture.

"Oh, sweet mercy," Ricky wheezed.

"Not the bird," Emily said. "The *bark*. At the base of the tree. Right *there*. See?" Ricky tried to examine the tree's base, but his gaze kept floating back to the menacing bird-of-prey. Emily pulled his chin back down until he finally spotted the object of her concern—several parallel cuts in the tree's bark. Five cuts, to be exact. Positioned in the unmistakable form of a claw. An exceptionally *large* claw.

BOOM!

"*AHHHHHHHHH!*"

The high-pitched squeal echoed in the air. Emily clamped a hand over Ricky's mouth. *"Shhh!"* She made him swallow the remainder of his scream before releasing him. A heavy rain started to cascade down on them.

Emily gave Ricky an irritated look. "No."

"But I didn't say anything..."

"I know, but you *thought about* saying something and the answer is *no*. We can't leave until we rejoin the others. Otherwise, they'll think something bad happened to us."

"Something bad *did* happen to us!"

"Oh, shush." Emily rolled her eyes, as was her habit anytime Ricky opened his mouth. "Let's go!" They pulled their hoods low, tilted their heads downward, and left the claw-scarred tree and its sinister inhabitant behind. The sky illuminated with a flash of lightning, followed by the deep rumble of thunder.

They rounded the corner and found themselves standing before an expansive graveyard. Ricky's voice cracked. "The graves of his victims."

"Wow," Emily whispered. "You might actually be right about this."

"It's not the first time I've—"

"Oh, shut up," Emily snapped. "Stay here."

"Wait! What are you doing? Why am I staying behind?"

"Because you're too noisy," she said, swatting him away. "Now *shhh*!" Ricky watched her enter the graveyard as though taking the long march down death-row to the execution chamber. He looked to his left, searching for James and Catherine. The sooner they arrived, the sooner they could all leave this horrible place.

"*AHHHHH!*"

The scream cut through night.

Ricky spun back to the graveyard—but Emily was gone.

Into a House of Horrors

A scream echoed in the night.

James cranked his neck. "Did you hear that? That sounded like..."

"Emily," Catherine finished. "Hurry!"

They reached the backyard, but saw no sign of Ricky or Emily.

James looked down as Catherine tugged his sleeve. "What?"

She didn't answer. *Couldn't* answer. She pointed to the graveyard. Straight ahead, between the tombstones, someone—or some*thing*—was coming toward them. As the figure, only faintly visible in the haze, staggered slowly forward they realized it was holding an axe.

Catherine latched onto James' leg tighter than a freshly

washed pair of blue jeans. The phantom raised the axe over its head and charged. James wanted to run, but was held in place by both fear and Catherine's dead weight. The shrouded figure released a savage bellow and swung the axe.

James rediscovered his wits just in time to duck. The blade sliced over his head, nipping the tips of his spiked hair. The axe came swinging down again, and this time he wouldn't be fast enough.

"Stop!" Catherine yelled. The axe head stopped an inch from James' sweat-covered nose.

"*Catherine? James?* Is that *you?*" The axe-wielding phantom was, in fact, only Ricky. James stroked his hair, inspecting the aftermath of his near-fatal haircut.

"You almost cut my head off, you lunatic! What in the world were you thinking!?"

"Emily is gone," Ricky whispered.

"Gone? *Where?*" James seized his brother's shoulders and shook him. "Richard Daniel Cavanaugh, snap out of it! What happened?"

Ricky extended his arms in a gesture of helplessness. "I don't know. We found claw marks on the tree and a ridiculously large bird that wanted to eat me. Then we found this graveyard. She told me not to follow. I'm too noisy, she said. I didn't agree, of course. I'm as quiet as a ninja when I want to be. Sometimes I even..." Another firm shake snapped

Ricky back into focus. "Emily walked into the graveyard. I looked away. I heard a scream and then she was gone."

"What do you mean...*gone*?" Catherine asked.

Ricky scowled. "I mean *gone*. There aren't many possible meanings for the word *gone*. She vanished. *Poof.* I raced to save her but was too late. I found this axe sticking in the dirt. When I saw you in the fog, all covered in cobwebs and stuff, I thought you were the bad guy."

"You said something about claw marks?" James asked.

Ricky nodded. "Big ones."

"We need to go home," Catherine declared in a bird-like chirp. "We shouldn't have come here." Without waiting for a response, she turned and bolted.

"Cat, wait!" Ignoring them, she vanished into the fog, running as if the sky were falling and their house was the only safety bunker. James looked to Ricky. "We can't let our baby sister go alone."

"What about Emily? We need to rescue her!"

James grimaced. "I know, but...well...maybe Emily just got lost. She's probably already halfway home."

"Or maybe a savage monster is about to eat her limb by limb!"

"Yes, or that," James said, conceding to the more likely possibility. He glanced at the house, then back to Ricky. "Sorry, bro!" He spun on his heels and followed Catherine into the mist. Ricky found himself standing, a graveyard behind, a house of horrors ahead, and very much *alone.*

His knuckles turned white as he squeezed the handle of the axe. He clung to the weapon as if his life depended on it—which it very well *might.*

He took one small step.

Then another.

Then another.

He arrived at a narrow flight of stairs. At the top of the stone steps was a wooden door. Ricky considered his options. **Option One:** Follow James and Catherine to safety, but abandon Emily to be eaten by monsters. **Option Two:** Heroically attempt to rescue Emily, but likely end up as the evil creature's tasty midnight snack. The icy rain slammed against his face as he weighed the two choices. Finally, with a resolute nod, he ascended the steps toward the door.

Even if the night ended in a slow, grisly death, his decision had been made. He would rescue Emily or die trying. The wood door was freckled with holes, no-doubt housing a legion of sizable termites. *It's probably locked,* Ricky thought. He grabbed the doorknob and twisted. The door glided slowly open.

Creeeeeeeeeeeak.

With a final, feeble gulp, Ricky stepped into the haunted house.

That Feeling of Being Watched

Ricky ventured forward, guided only by the ashen moonlight leaking in through the open back door. The room was empty aside from a single desk in the corner. The chamber's walls were a different matter entirely. Every inch, from floor to ceiling, was covered with framed paintings.

It was impossible to discern any of their details. Looking closer, Ricky realized why. Every painting was coated in a thick layer of dust. All except for one. The painting stood out like a sparkling new Ferrari in a used-car lot. The lack of gunk and grime suggested it was newer than the others.

The painting depicted a simple, two-story house. Ricky was an atrocious artist but had seen enough of Emily's artwork to recognize excellent quality when he saw it. The painting was so life-like it looked more like a high-definition photograph than paint on a canvas.

There was something strangely familiar about the image. *Had he seen it before?* He leaned closer. Then it struck him. He had never seen the painting, but he *had* seen that house. In fact, he lived in it.

Panic swelled inside as he looked through the window of his own bedroom. He could see the hockey poster hanging beside his messy closet. A poster he had hung just two days ago. He noticed a red splotch on the doorstep. His blood-soaked shirt. *Impossible!*

He scooted away from the painting as though it were a grenade with the pin pulled. The artist, whoever he was, had been watching him disturbingly closely. *But why?* Ricky wasn't sure he wanted to know the answer. He needed to find Emily. Now more than ever.

Creeeeeak...Creeeeeeak...Creeeeeak....

The wooden planks of the ceiling bowed and dust showered down, coloring his brown hair gray. Someone was walking on the floor directly above him. Ricky listened closer. Judging by the way the ceiling boards bent, it seemed that there were *two* people walking overhead. *The killer has Emily!* Time was running out. Ricky sucked in a mammoth breath, raised to his tip-toes, and scurried to the next room. *Quiet as a ninja, indeed.*

The strained light from the back door was now too faint to be of any use. Only a solitary oil lantern provided some meager illumination. Ricky found himself in the kitchen. His eyes were immediately drawn to an array of objects strewn across the counter. The lantern's light glimmered off their metallic surfaces. Knives. Not simple butter knives, mind you. They were gargantuan butcher's knives. The type used for sawing through particularly thick slabs of meat. *Or trespassing teenage boys*, Ricky thought with a lumpy gulp.

He realized that the footsteps overhead had stopped. *I can't dilly dally*. Before he could take another step, however, an intense odor filled his nostrils. The scent was musky...like the damp fur of an animal.

A soft growl sounded from behind.

Ricky spun to see a menacing shape looming over him. The light glimmered off a set of sharp fangs. The outside wind howled and a forceful gust burst through the open back door, snuffing out the lantern and slamming the door shut with a *bang*.

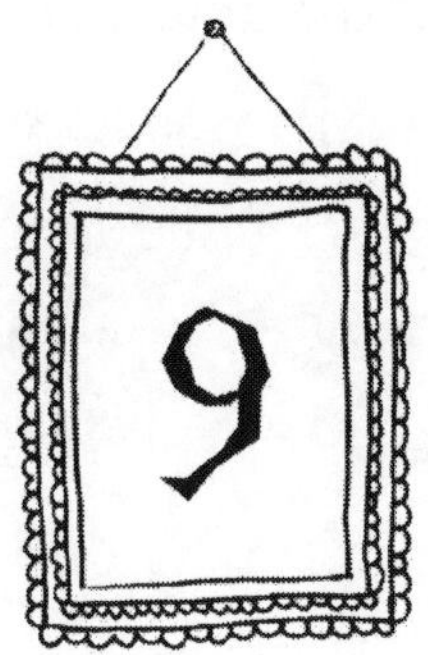

Tonight's Dinner is Teenage Boy

Ricky plunged into total darkness. He had no bearing on the direction of the kitchen's exit or, more importantly, the location of the ravenous monster. At any moment Ricky's bones would crunch like dry twigs as he was eaten alive.

The good news—the feral beast growled again, revealing its position. The bad news—it was directly behind him. Ricky felt the warmth of the creature's putrid breath against his neck. He lunged forward, and felt a gust of air as the monster's snapping jaws narrowly missed him.

Ricky slammed into the kitchen island with a grunt. The collision wrenched the axe from his hands, sending it *who-knows-where* into the pitch-black room. Still blind, Ricky climbed onto the island and dropped down on the other side. In the process he kicked an array of unseen tin objects that clattered to the floor. If the killer upstairs wasn't already aware of his presence, he certainly was now.

At the moment Ricky had more pressing matters to fret about (namely, how to not be torn apart by razor-sharp fangs). The monster's claws ticked against the floor as it circled the island. Ricky tried to make a mental map of the kitchen. If he could remember the location of those large knives, he could use them to slay the beast. Another husky growl made Ricky resort to Plan B: *RUN FOR HIS LIFE!*

He dashed forward and—*CRASH!*—slammed face-first into a wall. *Ouch!* The chase, brief as it had been, was over. There was nowhere to run and no way to defend himself. He could do nothing but wait, offering his gangly body as a late-night snack for the child-devouring creature.

The ticking of the creature's claws grew louder.

ClickClickClickClickClickClickCLICKCLICKCLICK!

Ricky waited.

The beast howled.

Ricky wondered if the monster would enjoy the taste of his limited-edition coco-scented deodorant.

CLICKCLICKCLICKCLICKCLICKCLICKCLICKCLICK!

Then, out of the corner of his eye, Ricky saw the most glorious sight he'd ever seen in all his thirteen years of life—light! It flickered in the distance, faintly exposing a doorframe at the end of a short hallway. The corridor had been invisible from where he had been standing, but now appeared like a white knight galloping in to rescue him. Ricky sprinted toward it.

BANG!

The room rattled as the monster crashed into the wall where Ricky had just vacated. Ricky's arms swung wildly, propelling him forward. The monster bellowed and gave chase. Ricky passed through the open doorway and spun around. The light illuminated the charging creature, reflecting off its white fangs. The beast pounced.

Ricky slammed the door with all his strength and locked the deadbolt.

THUD!

The collision launched Ricky to the floor. He propped himself onto his elbows, not daring to move or even breathe. He waited for the creature to ram the door again—but nothing happened. Ricky exhaled in relief.

He surveyed his new surroundings. The dancing flame of a hundred candles lined the walls, stretching down an almost endless hallway. At the far end, scarcely visible in the distance, was a lone door. Ricky obviously couldn't return the way he'd come. That left only one option. He began walking toward whatever lurking horror awaited him at the other end of the hall.

Meeting Your Nightmare

The narrow passageway seemed to stretch to infinity. No matter how many steps Ricky took, the door at the far end never appeared any nearer. It was as if some dark spell had been cast over him, forever trapping him on an unending treadmill. As with the previous room, the walls were plastered with hundreds of paintings. The house's inhabitant might be a psychopath, but he appeared to be a *high-cultured* psychopath.

A haze of dust swirled in the air. Ricky sneezed. The sound exploded down the hallway like a trombone blast. He cranked his neck, glancing at the door behind him. *How long would the lock keep the monster out?* The obvious answer was: *not nearly long enough*. Ricky increased his pace.

Eventually, after what felt like an eternity, he reached the end. The door was slightly ajar. *I'm crazy. I'm crazy. I'm crazy,* Ricky thought, then poked his head through the narrow crack and whispered. *"Emily? Are you in here?"*

No response.

He pressed the door open another inch. "*Emily?*"

Still no answer.

He pushed the door open the rest of the way and stepped inside. Floor-to-ceiling bookshelves lined the walls of the oval-shaped room, housing countless tattered tomes. From the high-roofed ceiling hung an enormous chandelier, wielding at least fifty lit candles.

"Emily? You in here?" With every call, his voice grew more timid and less audible. He ventured deeper and deeper into the musky room. Under normal circumstances, a room full of dusty old books would be heaven for Ricky, but the

current situation made him feel that it was very much *the other place.*

He tried to call for Emily again but only managed to produce a wet, frog-like croak. *Well,* he thought. *No one can say I didn't try.* As he turned to leave, the door suddenly glided closed.

Creeeeeeeeeeeeeak.

Click.

Ricky stared stupefied at the closed door. *Well that was certainly…unnatural.*

He heard a crackle and felt a wave of hot air brush against the back of his neck. He slowly turned. A blazing fire now filled the fireplace and, standing before the dancing flame, was a tall man. The man spoke in an eerily soft rasp.

"Welcome to my house."

An Unexpected Introduction

The man looked as ancient as the house he lived in. His wrinkled skin had a sickly gray hue and stringy snow-white hair hung down his back. An abnormally large nose curved like a fishhook over his rotted, yellow teeth. The man's gnarled hands gripped a cane for support. Ricky recognized the two piercing green eyes below the man's bushy eyebrows.

"You must be tired," the man said with a voice so gritty it made sandpaper seem like a feather pillow. He motioned to an empty chair beside the fireplace. "Please, have a seat."

Ricky didn't move. He stared at the stranger without blinking (or breathing, for that matter). The offer was obviously a trick. The moment Ricky sat the man would strike like a coiled cobra.

"Where's Emily?" Ricky demanded, feeling no bigger than a grasshopper. Even hunched over against his cane, the man was several feet taller than him. The stranger's chapped lips curved into a devilish grin.

"Is that her name? She wouldn't tell me."

A hot pain burned in Ricky's chest. "What have you done to her? You criminal!"

The man tilted his head. "*Criminal?* Ironic, as *you* are the one currently breaking the law as a trespasser in my house. Although I *do* appreciate company for my late-night tea." He strode across the room to a round table. "Do you prefer black or herbal? No worries. *Both* are caffeine free. I always find a cup of hot tea soothing before bedtime." He set to the task of making the tea, apparently taking Ricky's silence as a *yes*.

Ricky remained perfectly still. His imagination had concocted many horrifying possibilities of what he'd encounter inside this haunted house. Being offered a cup of herbal tea by an elderly man had *not* been one of them.

Finished preparing the tea, the stranger hobbled back to the fireplace. He set the cups on a table and gingerly lowered himself into one of the chairs. Pressing a cup to his lips, his entire body wiggled like a wet dog as the hot liquid flowed down his throat.

"Jeepers, creepers!" he exclaimed. "You'll want to let it cool before drinking. Wouldn't want you to burn yourself." A wheezy laugh exploded from his mouth, as though he'd just delivered the world's most hilarious joke.

"Emily," Ricky said again, mustering the last of his courage. "What have you done to her. Is she...is she...*dead?*"

A mortified expression gripped the man's face. "*Good heavens!* Of course not! What do you think I *am*? A maniacal murderer or something?"

Ricky rubbed a foot against the back of his leg. "Well, actually..."

The man waved a hand. "Oh never mind that now. Come, come. Your tea is getting cold." Fearing that he didn't have a choice, Ricky sat in the empty chair. He felt like he would melt into a steaming puddle of goo from the intensity of the man's scrutinizing gaze. Arm trembling, Ricky took a sip of the tea.

"It's good," he said, stuttering his words. The stranger smiled and relaxed in his chair, apparently satisfied.

"I grow the tea leaves myself. Out back. You probably saw some of my prized work on your way inside." An image of the foggy graveyard flashed into Ricky's mind and he wondered just what kind of *prized work* the hermit was referring to.

The stranger's eyes narrowed. Ricky glanced down and realized he was strangling the life out of his teacup with both hands. Panicking, he quickly released the mug. The tea sloshed onto the floor as the cup rolled across the room.

"I'm so sorry!" he blurted.

The stranger laughed. “No worries. Van Gogh will thank you for the gift.”

“Van Gogh?”

“Oh, forgive me. I assumed you must have met him on the way in.”

“Met who?”

“My puppy,” the stranger said, beaming with pride. “A cute little guy. Has a *killer* appetite, though.”

Ricky’s jaw went limp. “That *thing* in the kitchen was your *puppy?”*

“Of course. Who else would it be?”

Ricky wanted to yell *“A blood-thirsty demon that dines on the flesh of innocent young boys,”* but stopped himself. The room *had* been dark and darkness had a way of playing tricks on a terrified imagination.

“About Emily...” Ricky began, but the man cut him off.

“Of course, of course,” he muttered, as though annoyed to have teatime disturbed by such trivial matters. “She’s fine. Just a few scrapes and bruises and maybe the sniffles in the morning. Nothing a warm bed and warmer bowl of chicken noodle soup can’t remedy.”

The hope Ricky had given up for dead was slowly resuscitating. “Where is she? What happened to her? Can you take me to her?”

The stranger released a throaty chortle. “Easy now, lad.

She's on a sofa upstairs beside a warm fireplace. Last I checked she was sleeping like a baby. Seems she accidentally stepped onto one of the hidden trap doors. I really do need to put up some signs. Old house, you see. Some mumbo-jumbo nonsense about exits and fire-safety. Usually they're no problem, although Van Gogh gets stuck in one on occasion." The recollection produced another fit of breathy laughter.

"Can you take me to Emily?"

"*Now?*" The stranger appeared startled at the request. "But you spilled half your tea. Don't you want another cup?" He seemed to find Ricky's insistence on finding his lost friend instead of tea utterly preposterous.

"Thanks, but I really should be taking Emily home. It's late."

The old man sighed with obvious disappointment. "Very well, very well." He stood, using his cane for balance. "Come along." His feeble legs wobbled beneath the weight of his body as he hobbled to the door. Ricky trailed several feet behind. He still had that nagging feeling that the stranger was merely luring him like a pig to the slaughterhouse. Reaching the lengthy hallway, the old man lifted his cane and speared one of the paintings on the wall.

CRACK!

The wall broke. Or rather, it *opened,* spinning like a revolving door. The man flashed Ricky a toothy grin, then disappeared through the gap. Ricky glanced one last time down the long hallway, knowing full well that this was his final chance to run away, and then followed the stranger through the secret passageway.

The Painter and His Paintings

The house was a labyrinth. Ricky followed the owner around corners, up and down staircases, and through more secret passageways than he could count. He may as well have been dropped into the middle of the Sahara Desert with nothing but a bag of salty airline pretzels. If he ran now, he'd spend the rest of forever wandering aimlessly until finally dying of starvation and thirst. The more they continued to twist and turn through the ancient mansion, the more Ricky started to think starving to death in a distant desert might be a better fate than whatever diabolical plan the stranger had in mind.

The man came to a sudden halt. "Here," he wheezed. "Just as I said." Ricky peeked around the man, bracing himself for sights of unspeakable horror. He gasped. Across the room, resting on a sofa beside a crackling fireplace, lay Emily.

Ricky rushed to her side. Emily's mouth stretched into a

yawn and she rubbed her groggy eyes. “Ricky? Is that you? I had the most bizarre dream....” Her eyes went wide at the sight of the gnarled man in the doorway.

“It’s okay,” Ricky said. “You fell through a trap door. This friendly gentleman was taking care of you. We can go home now.” He spoke the last part more for the stranger than for Emily.

The man blinked several times, as if waking from a trance. “Oh. Of course, of course. *Goodness gracious.* Is that truly the time? Yes. Off you go. Home to bed. Yes, yes.”

Ricky helped Emily to her feet. “Sir, could you please show us the direction to the door?”

“Of course, of course. Just this way.” The man hunched over his cane and set off down the hall. Ricky and Emily exchanged worried glances, then jogged after him. As they went, Emily’s eyes were drawn to the paintings covering every wall.

“They’re *fantastic,*” she said with glimmering eyes. “These are the most beautiful works of art I’ve ever seen. Are you a collector?”

The stranger huffed. “Of course not.”

“But there must be *a thousand* paintings here!”

“Twelve thousand, three hundred, forty-one and three-quarters.” he said, his voice droning on as though reciting the most laborious pages of an algebra textbook. “The last one is still a work in progress, you see."

"Are you saying...." Emily shook her head. "No, that's impossible. Are you saying that *you painted* all of these twelve thousand, three hundred and...well...*all* of them?"

The stranger whirled around. Ricky and Emily tripped over each other to avoid crashing into him. "Of *course* I painted them. Could another artist have produced so many excellent works? *Bah!*" His entire body shook, as though the very thought disgusted him. "I suppose some like Michelangelo weren't *that* bad. But he never had enough courage to take his art to the next level. *Bah!* Amateur. Never mind that. Come. The exit is just ahead." He departed, still muttering to himself.

They hadn't gone far when something else caught Ricky's eye: a door. Not just *any* door, though. Every other door in the mansion was made of wood. *This* door was made of shiny steel. Also, whereas not even the backdoor to the house had been locked, *this* door was fastened shut by three thick, metal

deadbolts.

"What's behind the door?" he blurted.

The old man leaned forward, "*Secrets.*" Something about his tone sent a shiver down Ricky's spine.

"What kind of secrets?"

The man's grin deepened. "If I told you that, then they wouldn't be secrets any more, would they?"

"No, I guess not," Ricky muttered. After an uncomfortably long silence, Emily grabbed his elbow and pulled him toward the exit. "Thanks for your hospitality. We apologize for bothering you. We'll never disturb you again. We promise."

Alarm flashed over the stranger's face. "Nonsense! You're no bother at all. A pity we didn't have more time for tea! You *must* pay me another visit sometime."

"Sure," Ricky said mindlessly, anxious to escape the house.

"*Splendid!*" exclaimed their host. "Tomorrow. Shall we plan for just after dinner?" Before Ricky could protest, the man clapped his arthritic hands. "*Splendid!* I'll have the tea ready upon your arrival. Don't be late!"

Ricky's mouth opened and closed several times like a fish but no words escaped. Emily was equally dumbfounded. The man opened the door, letting in the chilly night breeze. "Sleep tight, my friends." He scratched at his chin. "Oh, and if you see Van Gogh out there, tell her to come home. She's made an awful habit out of escaping."

Ricky gagged. Another encounter with Van Gogh was the *last* thing he wanted. He followed Emily out of the house. The fierce rain had stopped but the ground was now covered with a thousand murky puddles. Ricky turned back to face the man standing in the doorframe, the moonlight reflecting off his colorless skin. "I'm sorry, Sir. You seem to know our names, but I don't believe we got yours."

The man's crooked grin returned. "Just call me The Painter."

The Painter watched the two frightened children scurry off into the night. They ran with the vigor of Olympic track runners. A large shape appeared at his side. He ran his boney fingers through Van Gogh's thick fur, drawing a satisfied moan from his pet. "Come, my lovely."

He wandered back down the corridor to the metal door. Reaching into his collar, he retrieved a necklace, from which hung a large, rusted key. He placed the key into each of the three deadbolts, one after another.

Click.

Click.

Click.

An intense aroma was released from the other side as he opened the heavy door. "Come, my lovely. We have work do to." He stepped into the room, pulling the door shut behind him.

Death On The Mind

His house was as quiet as a graveyard as Ricky crept inside. After fleeing Hallow's Drive he had walked, or rather, *run* Emily to her home a few doors down the street. The instant she shut the door he had sprinted back to his own home and crawled in through the back window.

He tiptoed up the stairs toward his bedroom. No light came from James or Catherine's rooms. As always, a cluster of Lego booby-traps was positioned in front of his sister's door. Had Ricky not been so horror-stricken himself he would have purposefully set off the traps just to see Catherine's alarmed reaction in the morning. For maybe the first time in his life, however, he had bigger worries than tormenting his little sister.

Ricky crawled into bed. The howling wind outside was fierce, blowing tree branches against his window like scraping claws. He pulled the blanket up just below his eyes and settled in for a long night of staring at the ceiling and contemplating his impending death.

The next morning, Catherine gawked at Ricky as though Superman had popped in unannounced to join them for a bowl of Cheerios®. He had just finished recapping last night's adventure. With each new detail Catherine's jaw seemed to melt farther toward the floor. If he didn't conclude the story soon she would trip over it.

"...and then he invited us back tonight for tea."

"What!?" exclaimed James and Catherine in unison.

Even Chevy, their one-eyed puppy, lifted his head in shock.

"And you said *not a chance*, right?" James sat up straighter, strangling the life out of his unfortunate breakfast spoon. "*Surely* you told him we wouldn't have tea with him until the day the sun rises in the east and sets in the west!"

Catherine lifted a finger. "Actually, the sun *does* rise in the east and set in the west."

James flushed. "Oh, whatever! My point is that Ricky *obviously* told the man no. Nadda. Never. End of story...*right?*"

"Well...you see...he was very insistent."

"You said *YES*?" Cereal-dyed milk was now cascading out of the corner of Catherine's mouth like water through a leaky bucket.

Ricky slumped into his chair until his eyes were level with the table. "Emily was there, too! Blame her! In our defense, we didn't actually *say* yes. We just sort of ran away."

James exhaled. "That's a relief. We just won't show up."

"That will only make him mad," Ricky said. "He's expecting us. You don't understand. This guy loves his tea. *Really* loves it. Like, more than Catherine loves ice cream."

A hush fell over the room.

Catherine grabbed her belly. Her stomach was twisting in knots from anxiety (or maybe it was just the mention of ice cream). "It's not a good idea to annoy a deadly killer. I don't have enough Legos to share my booby-traps."

"I've told you a dozen times," James said. "Your dumb traps are useless."

"Are not!"

"You're such a child," James said, straightening his posture to reveal all five-feet seven inches of his fourteen-year old frame (plus another half-foot if you counted the hair). "You two need to trust me as your leader. I'm the oldest and have had far more life experience than you."

"The only thing you led last night was running away," Ricky muttered under his breath.

James shot him an annoyed glance. "If this Painter guy wanted to murder us he could have done so last night." Ricky recalled the kitchen encounter with the man's *puppy* and wasn't convinced The Painter *hadn't* tried to kill him. "And, for the record," James added, "technically, *Catherine* led in running home last night."

Ricky and Catherine shared an eye roll as James stood, adopting the stance of a lecturing professor. "As the leader I have decided that it's not smart to annoy a deadly killer..." Catherine shook her head as James stole her words. "...therefore, our only choice is to return to Hallow's Drive tonight and have tea. Perhaps I can convince him that we're nice kids who don't deserve to be murdered. What do you guys think?"

"I think that's a horrible plan!" Ricky exclaimed. James scowled, but before he could respond, Ricky waved him off. "I know, I know. I'll understand when I'm a year older. Yadda, yadda, yadda." James closed his mouth, having intended to say just that.

Ricky licked his lips. "I guess we better live today as though it were our last day on Earth."

"I'm going to eat four tubs of ice cream for breakfast," Catherine said without the slightest hesitation. She grabbed a soup ladle and began to make good on her decision.

James brushed a hand across the towering spikes of his bleached-blond hair. "If I'm going to die tonight, I want my hair to look good at my funeral in case any pretty girls attend." His face went pale as his investigating fingers discovered a wilted hair spike. He dashed off to the bathroom.

Ricky found himself sitting alone in the kitchen. Even Chevy sauntered off to maximize his own Thursday, in likely the same manner he celebrated every other day—by finding hidden corners of the house to poop.

Ricky stared face to face with the most horrifying and grotesque creature he had ever seen. The droopy skin, spear-like nose, and demented smile forced Ricky to look away in revulsion. Just then, Emily pranced back into the room with a carton of paints in her hands.

"Ricky, if you came over here just to mope, then I'll have no remorse in kicking you out. *By force,* if necessary." History proved she'd be good on the threat; such as the time he'd foolishly chugged three energy drinks and proceeded to sing *The Little Mermaid* songs with a Scottish accent. "Seriously," Emily said. "You look distraught. You were brooding all through school today. What's on your mind?"

"Death," he muttered.

"Well," Emily chirped with exaggerated cheer. "Painting always gets my mind off my troubles." She stopped in front of the monstrous painting on the easel and squeezed an array of colors onto her palette.

"If you're trying to distract yourself from tonight's tea party then why are you painting that monster?"

Emily eye-balled him uncertainly. "What monster?"

Ricky pointed to the canvas. "That one! My goodness! The creatures from my darkest nightmares would run away in horror at the sight of that!"

Emily slapped his shoulder. "It's not supposed to be a monster! It's a portrait."

"*A portrait?* Of who?"

"Of *you*, silly!" She looked back to the painting, inspecting it with less enthusiasm than before.

Ricky frowned. "You think I look like *that*? Ouch!"

Emily huffed. "Portraits are the hardest paintings to get right. I *was* going to give this to you as a birthday present." She took a step back. "Oh, it's not *that* bad!"

Rick chomped on his lip to prevent a snide comment from exiting. As often happened when they were together, the day breezed by. By the time they finished dinner Ricky was feeling almost jovial. That is, until the dishes had been cleared and he remembered what the evening still had in store for them.

"I guess we should go meet James and Catherine. We don't want to be late," he said. At least, that's what he *tried* to say. What actually came out was a dump of nervous, nonsensical mumbling.

"Oh, come on. The sooner we go, the sooner it will be over," Emily said. "Just think, surely nothing tonight can be more terrifying than my portrait of you!" Ricky hoped she was right, but a flutter in his gut warned him that she was wrong. Very, *very* wrong.

A Different Sort of Familiar

"Follow my lead," James said, strolling confidently at the head of the convoy. "Let me talk to him *man-to-man.* As an adult, I'm far better equipped in these matters."

Normally Ricky would remind James that being fourteen-and-a-half didn't actually make him an adult, but all the moisture in his mouth had dried up like an apple slice under a hot summer sun. The *dry-mouth* epidemic was apparently extremely contagious as neither Catherine or Emily ventured to interrupt James' monologue either. Despite the eldest Cavanaugh's confident words, Ricky noticed copious globs of gel glistening in his hair. Indeed, his hair *would* look good if his funeral was soon-coming.

As though it had been dropped from the sky onto the horizon, the house at the end of Hallow's Drive suddenly appeared before them. The four children stood side-by-side (with James graciously giving up the convoy's lead), staring at their destination. Ricky scratched his chin. There was something strange about the house tonight.

The lawn was neatly groomed with a cobblestone walkway leading toward the front door. Had the old man found the time to do yard work since last night? Ricky scanned the scene further, still picking away at peach fuzz on his chin. Two stone lions stood atop pillars flanking the gate. He was *certain* that the statues had been frightening gargoyles, not lions. Ricky glanced at the others, but they didn't appear to have noticed anything unusual. He shrugged, and wrote it off as another example of the black-hole that was his memory.

James motioned to Ricky. "You and Emily were the ones The Painter personally invited, so it's only fitting that you two go first."

Ricky gave a soldier's salute. "Aye, aye, Captain!" Then muttered *"coward"* under his breath. He looked to Emily. "Ladies first, of course."

Emily rolled her eyes and walked through the gate toward the mansion. The others pattered after her like a brood of baby chicks. Reaching the door, Emily released a slow breath and grabbed the knocker.

Knock! Knock! Knock!

They waited.

Nothing happened.

Thirty seconds passed.

Still nothing.

"Maybe I should I knock again." Emily said.

James shook his head. "No-no-no. He's probably sleeping. It would be *terribly* rude to wake him." He pivoted on his heels and departed back toward the street. He had only advanced a few steps when a noise froze him—a soft growl.

"The Painter's puppy," Emily said.

Ricky's body went stiff. "That's no puppy. *Trust me*. The beast almost devoured me last night. It's a *monster*! At least five feet tall. With fangs the size of samurai swords." He tried to join James in the yard but Emily and Catherine snagged his arms.

The growling was joined by the sound of approaching footsteps. Ricky's sweaty hands looked like he'd dipped them into a jar of Vaseline. The footfall grew louder and the beast's howls became more animated.

They heard the deadbolt unlock.

Click.

The door knob slowly twisted.

"Guys, this is our last chance to run," Ricky croaked.

The door glided open.

Creeeeeeeeeeeeeeeeeeeeeak.

James and Ricky shrieked in harmonized, polyphonic yelps. Emily and Catherine shot them annoyed glances.

"*Shhh*!"

Ricky's nostrils caught the familiar whiff of musky animal fur.

The door finished opening.

In a blur of motion, the creature pounced through the opening. Ricky squeezed his eyes shut. His thirteen years of life flashed before him. *I'm too young to die! I've never even shaved!* The monster's warm breath washed against his leg and Ricky felt the cold, dampness of its tongue tasting his salty flesh.

"*Awwwwwwww*!"

The sound came from Catherine. Ricky peeked one eye open...and saw the most adorable puppy imaginable. The miniature ball of fluff, no bigger than a deflated football, wagged its tail as it slobbered over his legs.

"Remind me again," Catherine whispered, "how big were the fangs?" Ricky flushed. Had he really been so frightened last night to mistake this fur-ball for a flesh-eating monster?

A scratchy voice quieted them. "Welcome back." The Painter stood in the doorframe, his long gray hair pulled into a neat ponytail. "Come in. We don't want the tea to get cold." He turned, and pranced back into the house.

Catherine leaned in to Ricky. "You really *do* have as poor a memory as your report cards always say you do." Ricky titled his head. He could have *sworn* the man had been older. A hunched-backed elder with a cane. Maybe Catherine was right? Ricky shrugged and, with Emily leading the way, the four of them entered the house.

Sucked In

The long, twisting corridors became darker the farther they ventured into the mansion, as though they had been swallowed by a giant whale and were now being slowly guided toward its stomach.

"He's so talented," Emily said, examining the framed paintings that covered every wall. With no remaining wall space, numerous paintings had been pinned to the ceiling as well. "*Look.* It's perfect." The picture she had indicated was a replica of the Hallow's Drive mansion. Every detail, right down to the stone texture of the lion statues at the gate, was flawless.

The Painter led them deeper and deeper into the bowels of his large mansion. The soft pattering of Van Gogh's footsteps followed close behind as the puppy remained glued to Ricky's heel, giving his ankle a slobbery lick at every opportunity. Eventually they arrived at a small chamber at the back of the house. Several chairs were positioned in a semi-circle around the room's perimeter and, sitting atop a rickety table at the room's center, were five cups of tea.

"Please, please. Have a seat," The Painter said. "I've prepared a special Oolong Tea for you tonight. Had to journey all the way to a remote part of China for these tea leaves. Harvested them myself! Worth every drop of sweat and more!"

Retrieving their cups, they each took a seat. The Painter seemed oblivious to their apprehension. He launched into a meandering and exceedingly detailed story about the first time he had experienced this particular flavor of tea.

"*Ahem.*" James cleared his throat, bringing the dull narrative to a halt. "So, what do you do for a living, Mr..."

"Painter," the man finished. "Although obviously not *Mr.* Painter. What an absurd name *that* would be. No, no, no. *The* Painter will do just fine. Much more respectable."

James nodded, and glanced at the others. They only shrugged, as if to remind him that he had *insisted* they let him take the lead. Grimacing, James scooted forward in his chair. "So...um...I don't think I've ever seen you around Gallowood."

"I have no need to go into town." The Painter set his tea down and walked across the room to an intricately decorated chest against the wall.

"What about groceries? The movie theater? Gallowood Ranch? You must get bored spending all your time inside."

"Ha! Who said anything about staying in my house?"

James frowned. "Um. *You* did. Just now."

"Poppycock!" The Painter flapped his lips together and whinnied like a horse. "A man with a paintbrush can transport himself anywhere he could ever dream to go." He motioned to the surrounding paintings. "See? Look at all the places I've traveled! A painting is not just art. A painting is a *portal.*"

"But most people aren't as talented as you," Catherine said.

"*No one* is as talented as me!" The Painter returned to the center of the room with a bundle of supplies in his arms. "Which is why I'm going to teach you."

"Huh?" asked four voices at once. It was only then that they recognized the contents of his bundle: four easels, four canvases, a carton of paints, and a handful of brushes.

"Sir, we appreciate your offer," Ricky said, "but it's already late and we should be getting home."

"Nonsense!" Emily said, jumping up. "I would *love* to learn from you! Your paintings are incredible. Every one is a masterpiece!"

The Painter chuckled. "You're too kind. I mean, yes, they *are* incredible. But I'm still working on my great masterpiece." He motioned to the newly erected painting stations. "But enough about me. Let's begin!" Realizing that the old artist wasn't going to take no for an answer, James, Ricky, Catherine, and Emily took their positions.

"Now for the paint!" The Painter announced with a dramatic flare. He squeezed an array of colors onto their wooden palettes. Reaching Ricky, he frowned. "Drats! These paint bottles are empty. I'll go grab some others." The Painter spun on his heel and dashed from the room.

The four children formed a quick huddle. "What in the name of Ricky's oversized elf ears are we doing?" Catherine asked, clawing at her cheeks.

James nodded. "Cat's right. Yesterday we were convinced this dude was a crazy murderer. Now we're drinking tea and taking his painting class?"

"*You guys* were convinced he was a murderer," Emily corrected. "He seems like just a lonely old man enjoying some rare company."

Ricky scratched his head. "What about the graveyard? And the claw marks on the tree? What if he's just putting us at ease before he..."

"Before he does what?" asked a chipper voice. The Painter had returned and had stuck his head into their huddle.

"Nothing!" they all blurted at once.

He eyeballed them suspiciously. "Well, then, less chatter! More painting!" He squeezed fresh dye onto Ricky's palette. "Now *begin*!"

"Wait. What are we supposed to paint?" Emily *always* used a photograph as a reference. Painting without one was like a blind man trying to put together a two thousand piece jigsaw puzzle without using the image on the box.

"Whatever you desire most," The Painter said. "Whatever your imagination is whispering for you to create. Don't resist. Let your mind soar. Unleash your creativity. Let your dreams fly above the clouds."

Emily stood several feet away from her canvas as though it were contaminated with the Black Death. "That sounds fun and inspiring and stuff," she said, her voice becoming testy. "But what are we *supposed* to paint?"

Ricky bit his lip and entered into a staring contest with his own blank canvas. Farther down the row Catherine had already stroked the crude outline of a cheesecake, apparently taking the *whatever you desire most* suggestion literally.

Beside her, James had found no difficulty in selecting the perfect object to paint: *himself.*

Ricky peered at his canvas. He thought back to the last school fieldtrip to an art gallery. The modern paintings exhibited there looked similar to the creations he and James had drawn on their parents' bedroom walls with crayons as kids. *How hard can it be?* He decided to randomly slap down several globs of paint and call his creation *The Meaning of Life*. Satisfied with the idea, he grabbed a thick-bristled brush and dipped it in the red paint. *Here goes nothing*. He pressed the brush to the canvas.

Instantly, the whole room began to spin, churning faster and faster and faster. Ricky screamed as his feet floated off the ground. The white canvas rippled like a pond after a pebble had been tossed in. With a final startled cry, Ricky was sucked into the vortex.

The Creator of Worlds

Infinite white nothingness.

In every direction was an unending ocean of nothing.

Ricky floated, suspended above, well, *nothing*. The great white void had no top or bottom. There was no left or right. Upside down seemed no different than right-side up. In fact, Ricky soon lost track of which way *was* right-side up. He soared through the air but nothing changed. There were no landmarks to distinguish that he had left one location and arrived at another. He was no nearer or farther than before because there wasn't anything to be nearer or farther *from*.

Only infinite white nothingness.

Where am I?

The Painter's words echoed in his mind: *"A painting is not just art. A painting is a portal."* Had he been pulled into the painting? Was he now forever trapped in some unknown dimension? More importantly—how did this make *any* sense?

Ricky continued to drift weightlessly through the white abyss like an astronaut lost in space. He used to dream of defying gravity as a spaceman. In those dreams he'd always had a spaceship....

Color.

A single blue dot appeared amidst the nothingness.

The color slowly melted around his feet as if he were a candle that had been left lit for too long. More colorful shades materialized as the goo-like substance spread. Then, only seconds after it had started, it was over. Ricky looked around in astonishment. He was now sitting in the cockpit of a fully formed rocket ship.

The Painter's words repeated in his ears: *"Let your mind soar. Unleash your creativity. Let your dreams fly above the clouds."* Ricky had no idea what was happening but, whatever it was, it was totally awesome!

He combed his fingers through his shaggy hair. What good was a spaceship without a planet to land on? He decided on Mars. He shut his eyes and envisioned the crimson planet. When his eyes opened again the rocket ship was surrounded by rocky red terrain.

Is this really happening?

Ricky swam through the air down the corridor of the spacecraft. He yanked on the circular handle of the door but it didn't budge. He pulled harder. Still it wouldn't give an inch. *Hmmm.* With a simple wave of his hand a white splotch swiped across the door leaving behind no trace. Ricky realized with uncontainable glee, *I can do anything.*

He drifted through the now-empty doorway and landed on the rocky red soil. "I'm walking on Mars," he said aloud, as if to confirm what seemed way too epic to be real. Everything felt like a dream. Only somehow if felt more real than even his best dreams ever had.

He had unlimited power.

He was Ricky, *Creator of Worlds.*

There was nothing he couldn't do.

Let's make things interesting.

A green speck appeared in the distance. The color swirled like a dust-devil as it morphed into a tiny green alien. The rodent-looking creature had an utterly ridiculous looking fifteen legs and two triangular heads that were joined together by a single, beak-like nose.

Ricky stroked his chin. *Hmmmm, what else?*

A spotted tail sprouted behind the creature, capped off with a pink puffball at the end. Next appeared three bat wings. Ricky was curious to see if the alien could fly with an odd-number of wings. After all, *why not?* That he *could* create a creature so funny-looking seemed a good enough reason for him to do so. He had the power to do *absolutely anything.*

Endless possibilities jolted through his brain. He realized there were no stars in the sky. With a single blink a thousand twinkling lights ignited overhead. *Still needs a few minor adjustments.* He reached out and rearranged the stars like magnets on a refrigerator. Once finished, his newly-minted constellation formed a bright silhouette that had the uncanny resemblance of *him* (although he may have exaggerated *just a tad* on the over-sized biceps).

"RICKY?"

The sound blared from every direction at once. The voice belonged to Emily. Ricky suddenly remembered that he'd been painting with her and the others. He remembered a swirling vortex. The world around him began to spin. Everything began to fade.

Ricky rubbed his eyes. Instead of floating over Mars, he was in a dusty room with a flickering fireplace. Emily, James, and Catherine were staring at him with wide eyes and slack jaws.

Ricky took a step backwards. "What's going on?"

Emily's eyes narrowed into snake-like slits. "A good question. How *in the world* did you do *that?* Have you been lying to me all along? How *dare* you!"

"What are you talking about? I would *never* lie to you." Ricky scrunched his nose, then added, "At least not without a good reason."

Catherine stepped forward to stand by Emily's side. "Why didn't you tell us you were so good. I never in a trillion years thought I'd say this but, my goodness, you're a prodigy!"

"What are you talking about?" Ricky glanced past the two girls and noticed the row of canvases. Catherine's cheesecake more resembled a nuclear testing zone than something a sane human being would dare put into her mouth. Beside hers was Emily's. The colorful image of a mountain landscape adequately matched the picture in the open coffee-table book propped beside the painting. Next was James' self-portrait. The image looked something like an alien from a cheap horror B-movie. *An alien...*

Ricky turned to his own canvas.

His painting was amazing.

The red soil was perfectly textured. The bright metal of the spaceship glimmered. The stars overhead popped in the unmistakable shape of an unnaturally muscular teenage boy. Lastly, hidden behind a rock, was a bizarre three-winged alien creature. Ricky touched the still-wet paint just to prove the painting wasn't actually a photograph.

"How'd you do it?" James asked.

Ricky's mouth filled with saliva as he sought the elusive

answer. *How* had *he done it?* He was notoriously awful at art. Yet somehow he had gone *inside* the painting. He had been transported to a world where anything he could imagine was possible. Ricky felt a looming presence and looked up. The Painter's wrinkled face gazed down at him with fierce green eyes.

"Don't forget to sign your initials in the corner," The Painter said in a voice smoother than silk. "A painting is never finished until the artist claims it as his own." The old man's lips curved into a knowing grin.

The Most Talented Boy Who Ever Lived

He was going to be ridiculously rich. He would use $1,000 bills as scrap paper to jot down house chores and then hand them to one of his butlers to carry out. The paparazzi would be all over him. Mobs of beautiful girls would chase after him, squealing for a single glance of the world-renowned artist: Ricky Cavanaugh—the most talented boy who ever lived.

Ricky couldn't help but strut with a puffed-out chest. His mind was already racing with ideas for his next astonishing masterpiece. The possibilities were literally endless. The experience had been exhilarating. He desperately longed to return to that glorious white realm where anything was possible.

Not even Emily's vexed stare could dampen his mood.

Her face was glowing bright red as if steam would start flaring from her nostrils at any moment. She took pride in being better than him at everything. Getting her butt kicked at the one thing she considered her greatest talent was not going over well.

"You're *positive* you had no idea how good you were?" Catherine asked for what must have been the fifty-seventh time. Ricky hadn't told them of his bizarre experience within the white realm. A master craftsman never gives away his secrets.

"It wasn't *that* great," Emily snapped. "All *real* artists know that space pictures are among the *easiest* to do. I haven't painted something that unchallenging in *years*."

"How did you get the texture so perfect?" James asked, ignoring Emily. "I felt like I was actually in space just by looking at it."

Ricky shrugged, "Oh, it was nothing. You know, just putting paint down and stuff. I guess I just have a good eye for art." Ricky soaked in the admiring looks from his siblings. "Oh, yeah, I almost forgot. The Painter invited me back tomorrow night."

Emily's face morphed into a clump of wrinkles as her frown increased more than Ricky had thought was humanly possible. "Well, maybe this time I'll do something simple too, like silly planets and ridiculous aliens."

Ricky dropped his gaze. "Oh...um...Tomorrow isn't going to be another group lesson. The Painter invited me. *Just* me. You know, for a more advanced class. You weren't invited."

It turned out Emily's frown could increase after all.

Emily continued to glare at Ricky all through the next school day. So much so, that during gym class she failed to realize how close she was to the gymnasium wall while jogging laps. Only after she had been carried to the school infirmary did Ricky get a reprieve from her fuming. Not that he noticed, of course. He was far too preoccupied with thoughts of that evening's painting session.

He attempted several practice doodles, but the results were less than impressive (to put it mildly). No matter how hard he concentrated, he couldn't return to that glorious, magical dimension. The epic pirate ship battle in his

mind, when put onto paper, became a jumble of disproportionate stick figures standing atop unrecognizable polygons. The picture was so abysmal that when his teacher walked by his desk and saw it she hadn't even scolded him for doodling during class.

How had he done it yesterday? Had it just been dumb luck? Would he be able to do it again tonight? So lost in his thoughts was he that, despite several more artistic setbacks, the day raced by like a movie on fast-forward. He didn't say a word during dinner (not even to annoy Catherine). He merely looked straight ahead, mindlessly chomping away at his father's infamous *Macaroni Surprise* (which didn't actually contain a surprise of any sort), and watched the clock hands tick.

It was almost time.

Emily saw a silhouetted shape scurry past her window. The boy's hood concealed his face but she recognized the blue *Teenage Mutant Ninja Turtles* hoodie. It was Ricky. She pushed her window open, letting the cold evening air blow in. Tugging her own hood down to guard her face from the nipping breeze, she crawled outside and followed after him.

X Marks the Spot

The house at the end of Hallow's Drive was as desolate as ever. As Ricky passed between the two gargoyle guardians flanking the arched gateway, he hesitated for a brief moment. Hadn't those statues been stone *lions?* He gave a dismissive shrug and scurried through the weed-infested yard. Ascending the steps to the front door, he grabbed the knocker and gave it three raps.

Knock!

Knock!

Knock!

The door opened a crack and a head emerged like a gopher popping out of its hole. The Painter's stringy white hair swayed like dangling spaghetti noodles as he looked left and right. "Who goes there?" Spotting Ricky, his yellow teeth flashed a wide grin. "Oh, splendid! Come in, come in. I've already poured the tea...."

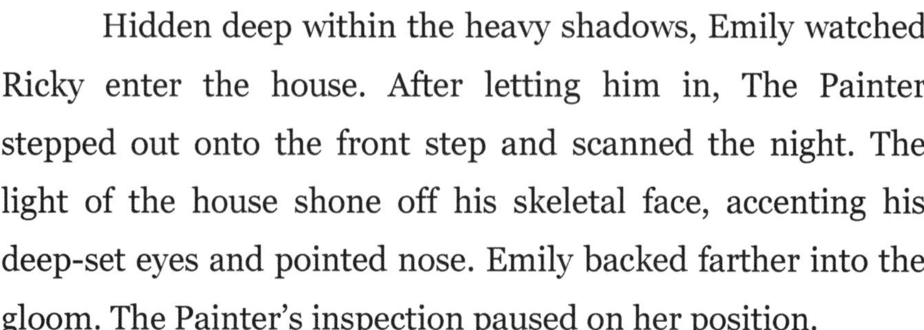

Hidden deep within the heavy shadows, Emily watched Ricky enter the house. After letting him in, The Painter stepped out onto the front step and scanned the night. The light of the house shone off his skeletal face, accenting his deep-set eyes and pointed nose. Emily backed farther into the gloom. The Painter's inspection paused on her position.

She released a soft yelp before quickly silencing it with her hand. The Painter's stare remained steadfast. Emily's face turned a shade of purple as she held her breath. After what seemed like forever, The Painter finally turned and disappeared into the house, flipping the lock and pulling the door closed behind him.

Emily exhaled.

Had he seen her? What had he been looking for? Did he know she had followed Ricky? Emily knew she was probably overreacting. Even so, she was convinced there was something sinister going on and she was determined to figure out what it was. Lowering into a crouch, she scampered through the shadows toward the back of the house.

Ricky's face beamed with pride. Displayed proudly on the wall, right alongside The Painter's own works, was his space masterpiece from yesterday. His *magnum opus*. Exhibited on The Painter's wall like an equal. Ricky noticed that the others' paintings were nowhere to be seen. *Amateurs,* he thought.

Unsurprisingly, two steaming mugs of tea sat on a table beside the two easels. The Painter swooped around Ricky like a raven, which was fitting, as he was dressed entirely in black, from his fluffy black slippers to his black bow-tie. "Are you ready to let your imagination soar?"

Ricky nodded eagerly. "More than anything."

The Painter leaned forward, his hooked nose harpooning toward Ricky's forehead, causing his eyes to cross. "You have not even *begun* to understand the limitless potential of art. A single painting can change the world, if only its painter is courageous enough to wield a brush and allow his imagination to *bleed* onto the canvas." He let the words hang in the musky air, then tapped the blank canvas with his cane. "Tonight you will be painting people."

"Like a self-portrait?"

"No!" The Painter growled.

Ricky was startled by the ferocity of the response. The Painter shook his head. "Not yet. A portrait is the most difficult painting to master." Ricky remembered Emily saying something similar. The Painter rubbed his hands together. "Golly, this old man's memory has become maddeningly leaky of late. I've forgotten your paint again." Ricky's eyes fell on a carton full of paint bottles stacked against the wall, but The Painter was already hobbling toward the door. "Be back in a jiffy."

Emily's breath fogged the air as she spied the backyard. Actually, it wasn't just her breath—the entire ground was blanketed by a white mist. Faintly visible through the haze were the row on row of weathered tombstones. She crept toward them. Halfway across the open yard her foot stepped on a dead twig.

SNAP!

Her heart skipped a beat. She remained completely still until she was certain the noise had gone unnoticed, then continued forward. She moved slowly, careful to avoid stepping on another branch or any of The Painter's hidden trapdoors.

The thick fog seemed to cluster around her ankles,

spiraling up her legs like wispy tentacles. She stroked the surface of the tombstones as she moved between them. The stone markers were brittle and their engravings faded beyond distinction.

Who is buried here? The house was old. It wasn't uncommon for ancient buildings to have graveyards, was it? Emily took another step...and lost her balance as the ground disappeared beneath her feet.

She grasped onto the nearest headstone for stability as her shoes sent dirt trickling into a pit that had been concealed by the fog. There was no mistaking the rectangular hole—it was an empty grave.

She grabbed a handful of dirt from a pile beside the tombstone, letting it spill between her fingers. The dirt was still fresh. That could mean only one thing—The Painter intended to add another dead body to his collection...and *soon.* There was no time to waste. More determined than ever, Emily advanced deeper into the dark cemetery.

One of the grave markers caught her attention. It was better preserved than the others. She knelt down, her knees sinking into the dirt, and wiped her hand across the tombstone. A cloud of dust scattered, revealing an inscription:

Fredrick Flaymore

She traced the letters with her finger. *Who was Fredrick Flaymore?* She didn't know anyone in Gallowood named Flaymore. Her finger jammed against another carved ridge directly after the name. An X. The letter didn't seem to fit with the others, as though it had been added later with a cruder tool. Her mouth went dry as the pieces of the puzzle connected in her mind. It was *a symbol.* As if something—or some*one*—had been crossed off a list. Her heartbeat quickened as she realized the truth—Fredrick Flaymore had been *murdered.*

She clasped her mouth as her eyes scanned the sea of tombstones. *I need to get Ricky out of that house!* She turned to run but crashed into something large. She looked up, straight into the haunting eyes of The Painter.

The fog wrapped around him like a billowing cloak and the pale moonlight reflected off crooked teeth exposed in a devilish smile. "X marks the spot," he whispered in a voice as airy as the cold evening breeze.

"*You*," Emily croaked. "You killed this man. You're a murderer."

The Painter stepped forward, and slid his tongue across his unnaturally thin lips. "Perhaps."

Emily tried to back away, but instead of solid ground her feet found only empty air. She stumbled backwards, arms flailing for anything to break her fall. Her left hand grasped the tip of the man's ponytail, plucking a thick handful of hair from his scalp. Her other hand reached for the man's face. Warm blood splattered down her arm as her fingernails cut into his flesh. She landed on a bed of soft ground. Dirt walls rose all around her, six feet high. She had fallen right into the empty grave.

The Painter looked down at her, five bloody gashes across his forehead from where she had clawed him. He lifted a shovel full of dirt.

"Goodnight, dearie."

Emily's screams were suffocated by the dirt as she was buried alive.

The Pirate's Life for Me

Ricky lifted his head as The Painter returned after what had seemed like an exceedingly long time. Several droplets of sweat dripped off of his pointed chin. "Sorry for the wait," he muttered. "I had to...mix the new paint."

Ricky nodded. "Shall I begin?"

"Yes, but there are two important rules." The Painter lifted his index finger. "*First,* don't under *any* circumstance attempt to paint *yourself.* You're not ready for that. *Second,*" he raised another finger, "do not paint anything *current.* A painter must look back before he can look ahead. A master artist can bring the past *to life.* Do you understand?"

Ricky nodded although, in truth, he hadn't been paying attention. All he had heard was, "Yadda yadda, mumble-mumble-mumble, something-yadda-mumble, *READY TO PAINT SOMETHING AWESOME AND BECOME SUPER*

FAMOUS?!"

The Painter motioned to the canvas. "Let your imagination soar. Never forget—a painting is not just art. A painting is *a portal.*"

Ricky dipped his brush into the paint. The thick dye dripped from the bristles as he pressed it against the canvas. The white surface rippled, the room started to spin, and Ricky was sucked back into the vortex.

Endless white nothingness.

He was back in the realm where anything was possible. That magical dimension where he—*Ricky Cavanaugh*—was ruler of everything. Where creating a universe was as easy as a thought and any dream instantly came true.

He stared at the unending white horizon and pondered what to create. He was like a child let loose in Willy Wonka's Chocolate Factory. When you had everything imaginable at your fingertips, how did you decide what to take first? Thankfully, Ricky was well-versed in the ancient "Code of Being a Boy." The code was simple: When faced with a choice, *bacon* and *pirates* are always good answers. With his stomach already stuffed with three helpings of Macaroni Surprise, Ricky picked choice B. He would create pirates.

He vaguely recalled The Painter's instructions. Something about not painting himself and only something in the past. The Painter had not, however, restricted him from painting *someone he knew* from the past. Ricky figured there was no harm in that. Surely The Painter would understand the need for a reference point. More importantly, there was no chance Ricky could pass up the chance to see his Grandpa Henry as a pirate!

He rubbed his hands together, creating static friction between them. Then, like tossing candy from a parade float, he swung his hands outward. Bright blue streams shot out from them. He continued tossing balls of color until all around him, as far as he could see, was water.

Strolling across the surface of the waves, he glanced down to the ocean depths below. He stomped his foot. A gray blob burst from the bottom of his shoe, torpedoing deep into the water. The colored mass slowly expanded into a majestic humpback whale.

Ricky traced the air with his finger, outlining a pirate ship. He added a stickman at the helm. The silhouette was as atrocious as his earlier practice sketches had been—but *this time* would be different. With a single clap of his hands the outline burst into color. A moment later a magnificent ship was gliding across the ocean toward him.

Standing at the ship's helm was his beloved Grandpa

Henry. With a *few* minor adjustments, of course. His grandpa looked fifty years younger and sported both an eye-patch and a peg-leg.

As the pirate ship soared by, Ricky's buccaneer grandfather scowled and shook a cutlass over his head. "Arg! Be you some dark spirit of the deep? Know ye be trespassing on the sea of the Dread Pirate Henry!"

Ricky burst into uncontrollable laughter.

The real world spun into focus.

Ricky rubbed his forehead, dizzy from the abrupt change. He felt like his brain was doing a high-flying gymnastic routine inside his skull. When his vision finally cleared, he inspected the painting before him. It was, in his own humble opinion, a masterwork without equal. An astonishing achievement that made the *Mona Lisa* look like a toddler's crayon doodle. In short—it was *perfect.*

Shockingly, his teacher didn't seem as pleased. In fact, The Painter had the look of a man about to strangle whomever had the misfortune of being in closest proximity. As the only other human in the room, Ricky realized that he was the prime candidate to fill that position. His self-satisfied smile wilted like a two-week old bouquet of roses.

The Painter's voice cracked like a whip. "*What have you done?!*"

Ricky flinched. "I just painted a pirate."

The Painter's finger speared the painting, landing on the buccaneer captain. "I told you *not to paint yourself*!"

A chill rolled over Ricky. He had never seen his teacher so impassioned by anything (other than rare and exotic tea). The tension eased when Ricky realized the misunderstanding. "Oh, *him*! That's not me."

"He *looks* like you!"

Ricky nodded. "It's my grandpa Henry. Mom says we look alike. It's the chin I think."

At this, The Painter slowly deflated and the fire left his eyes. "Very well, very well." He jiggled, shaking away the rest of his anger. "The painting *is* impressive. Not many can master the skill of painting people so quickly. You have a bright future ahead of you. A *bright* future. Oh, and don't forget to add your initials. Remember, a painting is never truly complete until it bears the artist's signature." Ricky quickly painted ***R.C.*** in the bottom corner, happy to take credit for the marvelous work.

The Painter rubbed his nose, as if scrubbing clean a splotch only he could see. "Hmmm. Tomorrow is Saturday. Why don't you come by again after lunch? You're now ready to try a self-portrait. You will need to bring a photo for reference. It is important that the picture is *current*. Do you have such a photograph?"

Ricky thought for a moment, then nodded. "My family just had a portrait done for our church directory. James and Catherine are in it, too. Is that okay?"

"Perfect." The Painter said. "It's getting late. Allow me to guide you to the door."

Ricky frowned. He didn't *want* to stop. He wanted to keep painting all night. To spend every possible moment in that wonderful world of endless possibility. He now understood the thousands of paintings wallpapering The Painter's mansion. The experience was more addicting than cheese puffs. With great reluctance, Ricky followed The Painter out the room.

As they traveled through the labyrinth of hallways they once again passed by the strange metal door. Ricky slowed to a stop. The three deadbolts were unlocked and the door was slightly ajar. *In his hurry to get my paint, he forgot to close the door,* Ricky realized.

The Painter continued forward, muttering about why Chinese clay teapots are superior to Japanese cast-iron teapots, oblivious to the fact that his student had fallen behind. Ricky's curiosity took over. *Just one peek won't hurt anybody.* He pressed his eye to the door crack.

A Wild Imagination

The room was dark, with only a few scattered candles providing any light. The narrow chamber was like an over-wide hallway with the deepest quarters blotched out by shadows. Several paintings lined one of the walls, but Ricky couldn't make out any details. Against the other wall were shelves that held what looked like glass jars full of some dark substance. *Probably tea or paint,* he guessed. He leaned in for a better view. As he did, something in the back shadows of the room moved.

CLICK!

The door slammed shut.

Ricky leaped into the air and twirled around. The Painter towered over him, peering down with murderous eyes. A web of tiny blue veins sprawled across his face like an underground ant farm, amplified by his maggot-toned skin.

Ricky's mouth became sticky as he rambled. "I'm so sorry. I...um...I had to...um... tie my shoe." The Painter's stare lowered to Ricky's feet. In particular, to the two laceless slip-on shoes. Ricky gulped.

Surprisingly, The Painter merely smiled. "No harm done. This *is* a difficult house to navigate. Poor Van Gogh has gotten himself lost for days! Better stay close to me from now on." He motioned to the hall. "Shall we proceed?"

Ricky quickly shuffled down the hall toward the back door. Every heartbeat was like a clanging gong in his head. Had he actually seen movement in the room or was it just his wild imagination playing more tricks on him?

The Painter joined him at the door. "Hurry home now, lad. And don't forget to bring that photograph tomorrow."

Ricky nodded. "I won't. Thanks for the lesson."

The Painter chuckled. "Oh, you are too kind. It's *me* who should be thanking *you!*"

Ricky blushed as he tried unsuccessfully to conceal his raging pride. "Goodnight." He opened the back door—and screamed.

In the doorway, backlit by the moon, was a monster. The faceless creature's black skin was as clumpy as curdled milk. As the monster moved, pieces of its dark skin detached and fell to the ground like discarded snake's skin. It wielded a shovel in its hands like a club. The lumpy skin shifted, revealing a mouth. "Ricky! Get behind me!"

Ricky reached to slam the door but paused. "*Emily*? Is that *you*?" He looked closer and realized that the creature didn't have gloopy black skin after all—rather, it was covered from head to toe in *dirt*. His best friend was barely recognizable beneath the coat of grime. "What are you doing here? You're filthy!"

A mud-crusted hand grabbed his collar and yanked him out the door. "Stay behind me," she ordered. "This man is a murderer! He tried to *kill me* tonight!"

The Painter was heaved over against his cane, holding his chest and panting. "Good heavens," he said between ragged breaths. "You nearly scared the life out of me!"

Emily wiped a hand across her face but the action only smeared more dirt from her hand onto her brow. "You would know *all about* taking the life out of someone, wouldn't you? You buried me alive!"

"*What?*" Ricky put a hand on Emily's shoulder. "What are you talking about? How can you possibly accuse this man of such horrible, false things?"

"They aren't false," Emily said, exasperated. "*Look at me*. I'm covered in dirt!"

The Painter tapped his foot impatiently. "You obviously tripped while snooping through my graveyard. It wouldn't be the first time."

"I didn't *trip*," Emily snarled.

"But you *were* snooping, were you not?"

This time Emily had no response.

Ricky stepped forward. "Emily, what you say is impossible."

"What do you mean?"

"The Painter was with *me* the whole time."

"Are you sure? Did you actually see him the *entire time*?"

Ricky scratched his chin. "Well, actually, I suppose he *did* leave once to grab the paint."

The Painter jiggled the collar of his shirt. "My clothes are remarkably clean for a man who was frolicking in a dirty graveyard, wouldn't you say?" Once again, Emily was rendered speechless. She looked to Ricky for support, but he merely shrugged.

"He's got a point."

Emily's mouth slowly curved into a devious leer and she jabbed a finger at The Painter. "Before you pushed me into the empty grave I scratched your forehead." Her grin deepened. "You were wearing your hair in a ponytail, but now I see you're letting it hang loose to cover your forehead. Convenient, wouldn't you say?"

The Painter's eyes shifted to Ricky. "Your lady friend has a remarkably wild imagination."

"Actually, she doesn't," Ricky said. Emily had the imaginative range of an outdated calculator with an expired battery. It wasn't like her to make up such fanciful tales. "I guess there's only one way to know for sure. Can you please show us your forehead?"

The Painter's face drooped. "*Surely* you jest. I'm afraid that in my old age I've gained unsightly warts as quickly as I have these wrinkles. Is it not an old man's right to cover up such repugnant flaws?"

Emily snickered. "Nice try, you despicable murderer. We've got you cornered like a rat! The game is over. Show us your forehead." She aimed the shovel at him like a spear.

The Painter hesitated, eyes dancing between the two children, before finally sighing. "Very well, young lady. *You win*. But don't say I didn't warn you." He wavered for just a moment, then lifted his hair. They gasped at the frightening sight.

In the center of his crinkled forehead were two repulsive warts. Each mountainous bump was crowned with a tuft of thin hairs. Apart from the vile lumps, however, there was nothing to see—not even the slightest hint of a recent cut or scab.

Emily's jaw dropped. "That's impossible."

The Painter let his hair fall back to his forehead. "I believe someone owes me an apology."

Running Out Of Time

Emily wanted to kill Ricky. This was not an uncommon feeling. But on this *particular* night the desire for his demise had reached uncharted heights. Being completely covered in smelly dirt only added to her displeasure. There was also the small detail of her having just been *BURIED ALIVE!*

The experience had been straight out of a nightmare. Unable to breathe or move, she faced certain death. Come to think of it, she still didn't know how she'd escaped. Had Van Gogh inadvertently aided her while digging for bones? What she *did* know was that the strange hermit on Hallow's Drive was a vicious killer.

Emily refused to let Ricky walk her home. She couldn't believe the little weasel had sided with the psychopath over her! Even worse, he had *the gall* to suggest it was all *her* fault for sneaking around where she shouldn't. She snorted. *Why were boys such utter dimwits?*

If she was going to win against The Painter—and she *was* going to win—she needed better help. She needed another girl. First thing in the morning she would conscript Catherine and hope the idiot-gene was restricted to the male half of the Cavanaugh family. She squeezed her hands into fists. Things had just become personal.

Mr. Painter, you messed with the wrong girl.

Catherine was an easy ally to enlist. The promise of *proving Ricky wrong* was the only sales pitch needed (well that, and the guarantee of an ice cream celebration afterwards).

"I'm not sure how coming here so early on a Saturday morning will help us prove this Painter fellow is a bad guy," Catherine said as she and Emily ascended the steps to the town library. Emily pulled the doorknob but it wouldn't budge. "What's the meaning of this!?" She rattled the door again.

"It's only 6:30 a.m.," Catherine said through a wide yawn. "Look at the sign. The library doesn't open for another half-hour."

Emily released her grip. Perhaps she was just *a little*

overanxious. She plopped down beside Catherine on the steps to wait. "Have you ever heard the name *Fredrick Flaymore*?"

"I don't think so," Catherine said, thinking for moment. "Wait, wasn't he a finalist on that *America's Most Handsome Tap Dancer* show?"

"No, that was Henry Flanigin," Emily said.

"Oh, yeah. You're right." Catherine closed her eyes. "Sweet mercy, he *was* handsome."

"*Anyways*," Emily said, resting her head against the door. "This Fredrick Flaymore guy is most likely from here in Gallowood."

"And The Painter admitted to killing him?"

"Yes. I don't think he expected me to escape so he didn't worry about revealing his secrets. Bad guys do it all the time. Now I'm going to make him pay for that mistake." Emily motioned to the library. "That's why we're here. I want to check the town records for any mention of a Fredrick Flaymore."

She checked her watch, confirming for the twentieth time that the library was still not open. The wait was agonizing. The Painter was bound to strike again soon. The image of the empty grave was tattooed in her mind. The Painter didn't tell her who the grave had been meant for, but one thing was certain: They were running out of time.

Something Smells Fishy...Or is That Just Lunch?

The ***Open*** sign was still flickering on as Emily tugged Catherine through the library door. For a small town, Gallowood had a surprisingly large library. Endless shelves, ten feet high, stretched out in all directions. The upper-floor offered more of the same. Emily groaned. "Why in the world do people need so many books?"

Catherine gave her a death glare. "I'm going to pretend I didn't hear that."

Emily took three slow breaths. *Where to start?* She glanced to Catherine, who still looked disgusted by Emily's reading aversion. "Cat, you come here all the time. Where are the computer reference stations?"

Catherine's revulsion morphed into amusement. "Computer reference stations? Gallowood doesn't even have cellphone reception."

Emily groaned again. *Why does everything have to be so difficult?* She spotted the librarian reclining behind a *Help Desk,* her angular nose buried in a large book. The librarian peeked a suspicious, spectacle-covered eyeball over the top of the book as they approached. By the most generous estimation the woman was no younger than one hundred and fifty-two. Her lumpy skin sagged off her bones like a damp shirt on a clothes hanger, and not even Sherlock Homes would be able to locate a neck on the unfortunate woman.

"Precious dearies, it warms me little ol' heart to see kids such as yourselves with a love for books. On a Saturday no less!" Her toadish voice had the same pleasant quality as fingernails scratching down a chalkboard. She continued to croak, "I just got a fresh stock of paranormal romantic dramas. Have you read *Dead in Love?* Oh, dearies, you simply *must!* A vampire falls helplessly in love with a zombie, who, unfortunately, is already in a serious relationship with an ill-tempered garden gnome. All set against a thrilling steampunk dystopian backdrop. It's sure to be the next big thing!"

Emily rapped her fingers against the counter. "Sounds *breathtaking*. But we're just here for some old town records. You know, accounts of people and events from *back-in-the-day*."

The librarian's eyes narrowed. "Why would you want to

read something like *that*? Are you *sure* you're not interested in a supernatural love-tale? What about the recent bestseller *Love at First Bite?*"

"We're sure," Catherine said, although Emily noticed that she had jotted *Dead in Love* down on some scrap paper for later.

The librarian sighed. "The younger generations don't appreciate great literature anymore. *Very well.* Have it *your* way. The reference books are on the upper level, in rows 233 to 257."

"Thanks!" Emily was already dashing up the staircase three steps at a time, dragging Catherine behind her. Weaving up and down the aisles, they finally reached the prescribed rows.

Emily's heart sank.

Every shelf was brimming with countless thick books. Catherine's shoulders sagged. "These will take *years* to look through!"

Emily pulled up her sleeves. "Then we better get started."

Ricky yawned, glancing with groggy eyes at his alarm clock. ***10:47 a.m.*** A glorious aroma filled the air. His mother must be cooking some delicious fish for an early lunch before she ran errands. Ricky rolled out of bed, landing on the ground with a heavy *thud.* After a quick lunch he would be on his way to Hallow's Drive for his painting lesson. He couldn't wait. A feeling in his gut told him that something *big* was going to happen this time.

Twenty minutes later, Ricky swallowed the final bite of fish and wiped the profuse tartar sauce spillage from his lips. Lunch had been scrumptious. A perfect way to start what was sure to be a memorable day. One final task remained before he could leave for his lesson. He needed to find James.

Luckily there was no creature—human *or* animal—born during the last six centuries that was more predictable and easy to locate than James. As sure as two plus one equaled three, James could be found standing in front of the nearest or largest mirror.

Sure enough, Ricky found his brother at their parents' full-length mirror. James was in the middle of enthusiastically strumming an air guitar. Pausing, he flicked his head in the world's coolest head-nod and muttered in an unnaturally gruff voice, "Whaz' up, babe?" Apparently unsatisfied, James quickly rearranged some of his gel-drenched hair-spikes and repeated the routine several more times.

Ricky cleared his throat.

James released a high-pitched squeal and spun around.

His face ripened when he saw his brother. "What are *you* doing here?"

"I live here," Ricky said, impatiently. "Mom said you were the last one to have our church directory photo. She said you needed to confirm you looked *rockstar* enough before you agreed to let the public see it."

James pulled the crumpled photograph from his pocket. "Now leave me alone. I have important business to take care of." He gave Ricky one of his now-perfected head nods. "And, for the record, I *always* look rockstar enough."

Ricky shook his head. *He's hopeless.* He examined the picture. *Perfect.* Time to head to the lesson. He didn't want to be late.

Emily wiped sweat from her forehead. Dozens of opened books surrounded her on the floor. She and Catherine had searched all morning and late into the afternoon, stopping only briefly for a less than satisfying lunch of vending machine potato chips and candy bars. She didn't know how long had passed since that dismal meal but her growling stomach suggested dinnertime was already beginning to creep up on them. So far their exhaustive hunt had uncovered a detailed food inventory of every Gallowood town picnic since 1952, a riveting account of 1973's unusually warm spring, and the abysmal statistics of the Gallowood Hornets' record-breaking streak of twenty-four seasons without scoring a point. And those were, by a sizable margin, the most interesting tidbits they had found. Nowhere had there been mention of anyone named Fredrick Flaymore.

Emily looked over at Catherine, who was encircled by an equally mountainous pile of books. Emily's leg muscles ached from lack of use as she stood. "Any luck?"

Catherine's head shot up, her face blushing. "I couldn't help it!"

Emily frowned. "What do you mean?"

Catherine lowered the massive book archiving the *Gallowood Times* that she had been reading—or rather, that she *appeared* to have been reading. Behind the dusty archives book was a copy of *Dead in Love*.

"Catherine!"

Catherine threw her arms up. "We've been here *all* day and this research was getting *so* boring!" She waved the novel in the air. "And this book is gloriously juicy! I'm *definitely* on team Garden Gnome, although I suspect he might actually be a hobgoblin in disguise...." Her voice trailed off and she squinted to focus on the newspaper archive lying open on the floor. "Oh, my gosh!"

Emily cranked her neck, attempting to read the upside-down article. The breath caught in her throat. In big bold letters was written:

MURDER IN GALLOWOOD!

She dropped to her knees and yanked the book toward her. Catherine scampered to her side and they pressed their heads together to read.

Tragedy strikes Gallowood! Citizens are in mourning following the first-recorded murder in town history. The victim's body was found early this morning on the floor of the local Tea Shop. The suspect is still at large and considered extremely dangerous. Along with the bloody footprints leaving the shop, a paintbrush was also found at the crime scene. Police have concluded that the brush is the likely murder weapon. The murder victim, a 43-year-old male, has been identified as Fredrick Flaymore.

Catherine jumped to her feet and backed away from the book as if it were a stick of burning dynamite. "The Painter *is* the killer! This is horrible! What are we going to do?"

Emily's stomach twisted into a tight pretzel. "We need to warn Ricky. He's in terrible danger. Is he at home?"

Catherine checked her watch. "No. He said he was leaving this afternoon and would be gone all evening."

Emily felt her skin grow cold. "Leaving to go where?"

"To The Painter's house." Catherine grabbed her cheeks. "Oh no! He said today's lesson was going to be *extra special.*"

Emily brought her hands over her mouth. "The Painter is going to kill Ricky."

A Picture-Perfect Family (With a Few Minor Alterations)

The potent scent of orange-mint tea wafted down the hallway of the Hallow's Drive mansion. The Painter appeared to be in a particularly pleasant mood as he motioned excitedly for Ricky to enter. Ricky fingered the family photograph in his pocket to make sure it was still there. Then, breathing in the delightful smell, he followed the old man. Van Gogh trotted close behind, tail wagging, and tongue lashing out against his leg.

Ricky was eager to get started. He longed more than ever to enter the mysterious and exhilarating world inside the painting. All his life he had wished for something to make him special. Instead, he was doomed with the ancient curse called "*the middle child.*" James had flawless hair. Catherine had little-princess charm. Emily had artistic talent. And him?

Nothing. Nadda. Zippo. Zero. Donuts.

A few years back he'd tried his luck at community soccer. But dreams of being the next World Cup superstar were short-lived. Despite the team missing several kids due to chickenpox, the coach had elected the curious strategy of playing the entire game shorthanded rather than sub Ricky in—that coach also happened to be Ricky's father. Yep. Ricky Daniel Cavanaugh had been tragically born without a single talent. There was nothing whatsoever to make him special—until now.

He slowed as they passed the thick metal door. Unlike last night, all three deadbolts were securely locked. Something else caught his eye—faint blood-red stains on the door handle. Fingerprints. *Red paint,* Ricky realized. He dismissed the sight. There were more important things to think about, such as how amazingly awesome his next painting was going to be. He hated to use the words *magnum opus* prematurely—but his track record didn't lie.

They reached the fireplace room at the back of the house. As usual, a blank canvas had been prepared on an easel and a mug of hot tea waited on a side table. The Painter stood waiting. "Did you remember to bring the picture?"

Ricky pulled the crumpled photograph from his pocket. The Painter swooped in and snatched it from his hands, examining it with his emerald eyes. "Yes, yes. This will do perfectly." He returned the picture. "Tonight's lesson will be your trickiest painting yet. The process is no different, mind you, but it is *extremely difficult* to get people to look *just right*. It's the faces. Yes, very tricky. They must be *perfect* if the painting is to succeed."

He leaned forward, pressing his face only an inch away from Ricky's. "Hear me clearly. Minor alterations are acceptable, but you must paint the portraits *exactly* as you and your siblings are *now*. Not in the past. Not in the future. *Now*. Do you understand?"

Ricky nodded. "Sure, no problem."

The Painter licked his lips. "Painting portraits isn't easy, but the most difficult things in life are always the most rewarding. This is your chance to do the impossible. To create as you wish things were, not as they have to be." He tapped his boney fingers together. "A painting is history. Through paintings we determine how the world will be remembered. How *we* will be remembered. At the tip of an artist's brush is the power to shape the world."

The Painter was acting particularly odd tonight (which was saying a lot). He almost seemed to be speaking to *himself*, as if he had forgotten Ricky was even in the room. Ricky glanced at the photograph. He might as well get started. Dipping the brush into the red paint, he brushed the first stroke. The canvas began to ripple....

Huffing and puffing, Emily and Catherine sprinted down the street. By their rotten luck, Hallow's Drive was at the complete *opposite end* of town. Gallowood wasn't big, but every mile gave The Painter more time to gruesomely murder Ricky.

Emily grabbed Catherine's arm. "We need all the help we can get. You should go home and get James."

Catherine raised an eyebrow. "I'm not sure James qualifies as *help*. Nothing makes a bad situation worse quicker than James." When Emily continued to stare, Catherine sighed and muttered under her breath, "Don't say I didn't warn you." She veered off in the direction of their house. Emily didn't watch her go. There wasn't a second to spare. Dark storm clouds were forming on the horizon. Emily put her head down and ran.

A perfect replica of Catherine stood before Ricky, complete with her infamous snooty scowl. He examined her, double-checking that she matched her appearance in the photograph. She did—right down to the small birthmark above her top lip. Ricky was impressed. The Painter had obviously exaggerated the degree of difficulty. Either that or, more likely, Ricky simply possessed legendary talent. He rubbed his hands together and prepared to create James.

A voice stopped him. "What do you think you're doing?"

Ricky turned to see the painted Catherine clone glowering at him. "Did you just *speak?*"

Catherine folded her arms against her chest. "Of course I spoke. I am quite good at it. In fact, I have better grammar than you and I'm only *nine*!" Ricky pushed a hand through his shaggy hair. Just his luck. Even in painted form his little sister was an annoying brat. She continued to chatter. "Ricky? What are you doing? Ricky? Ricky? Hey, Ricky. Ricky? Richard?

Ricky? Ricardo?"

Ricky tried to ignore her. He traced James's silhouette with his index finger. The outline filled with color like water into a bathtub until a perfect copy of James was standing before him. The fake James looked around in confusion.

Ricky blinked.

His brother's eyes lit up as a full-length mirror materialized in front of him. *That should keep him busy while I finish the scenery,* Ricky thought. Unfortunately, the same could not be said about his sister. Catherine continued to blabber behind him. "Ricky do you ever stop being so rude?"

Ricky grated his teeth. "Do you ever stop *talking*?"

"I dunno, do you ever stop looking like two-week old roadkill?"

Ricky snapped his fingers.

Silence.

Catherine instantly stopped speaking—although not by choice. Talking was awfully difficult when you didn't have a mouth. Ricky recited The Painter's words: *This is your chance to do the impossible. To create as you wish things were, not as they have to be.* The Painter was right. His siblings might get all the attention in the *real* world, but right now they were in *his* world. In *here* he could do whatever he wanted. They were only paintings, after all. He grinned. Might as well have a little fun.

He brushed a hand over James' porcupine hair. As he did, the hair drooped and grew by several inches. His brother's eyes bulged as he inspected his new mushroom-cut (complete with a cute little ponytail on top). James' face looked as though he had just seen his best friend die—and, in a way, he *had.*

Next, Ricky turned to his little sister. Even without a mouth she seemed to scowl in ways that should have been biologically impossible. He scratched his head. Catherine didn't have any single trait that she obsessed over the way James did. Ricky thought harder. Meanwhile, Catherine continued to gaze at him with her odd mouthless frown.

Then it hit him.

He knew the *perfect* alteration for Catherine. Inside the painting's portal he finally had the power to do what he had wanted to do in real life far too many times to count. He clapped his hands. With a small splatter of white paint—Catherine vanished.

A wave of joy flooded over Ricky. If only for a few moments, he had reset the clock to a time when *he* had been the baby of the family (with all the glorious perks that accompanied such an honored position).

Last but not least. Ricky sucked in a deep breath—and blew. Color surged from his lips, splashing to the ground. The puddle began to bubble as a body oozed up from it, sucking the paint into it like tornado.

Then it was done.

Looking back at Ricky, like a mirror's reflection, was *himself*. Ricky examined his creation, realizing once again just how ridiculously handsome he was. He correctly positioned the painted versions of himself and James to match the poses of original photograph.

Perfect.

Emily placed her hands on her knees, struggling for breath. She had *finally* reached Hallow's Drive just as the sun dipped below the horizon, ushering in the night. Looking down the desolate street, she could only faintly make out the shape of the lone house at the far end. *Almost there.* A sickening feeling in her gut told her she was already too late.

The Truth is in The Stars

Ricky felt guilty as he examined the finished painting. Removing Catherine from the picture had been amusing in the moment, but now he felt slightly ashamed. He took a deep breath—and just like that the guilt was gone!

The Painter pressed his face close to the wet canvas, inspecting every detail. Ricky picked nervously at his nails, awaiting the master's evaluation. To *his* eyes, the work was fantastic in every way imaginable. He especially got a chuckle at James' ridiculous hair. His back stiffened as The Painter finished his scrutiny.

"You've passed the exam."

Ricky exhaled in relief. "Thank you! Wait...*Exam?* This was a test?"

The Painter nodded. "It was, and you passed. Congratulations."

"What do you mean?"

The Painter placed a hand on Ricky's shoulder. "I've been waiting many, many years for a suitable partner to help finish my masterpiece. The work that will be my life's crowning achievement. Today I've found that partner."

Ricky was sure he must have misheard. "Are you serious?"

"*Dead* serious. Tomorrow you will help me to finally complete my *magnum opus.*" A devilish smile formed on The Painter's face. "Together, you and I will change the world."

Emily dashed down the long street. The foreboding feeling in her stomach wouldn't go away. Something horrible had just happened. She was certain of it. If she broke into The Painter's mansion right now would she find Ricky's mangled corpse—a bloody paintbrush speared through his heart?

There was abrupt movement in the street ahead. Emily looked left and right but there was nowhere to hide on the barren street. Had The Painter eliminated Ricky and now come for the rest of them? Her heart pounded as the dark figure approached. If she *was* going to die, she would do so with courage. The shrouded man was now close enough to hear his breath, the rustle of his jacket, and...wait, was he *whistling?*

Emerging from the shadows with a gleeful skip in his step, was Ricky. He tilted his head in surprise at seeing her. "Oh, hi. What are you doing out here?"

"Saving your life, you crazy moron!" She grabbed his sleeve and yanked him toward her. "We need to get as far away from here as possible. Hurry! There's no time to waste!"

"What are you talking about?" Ricky pulled his arm free from her grip. "I have the most wonderful news. You won't believe it. The Painter has asked *me* to be his partner! Tomorrow I'm going to help him finish his masterpiece and..."

SLAP!

Emily smacked him across the face. "Wake up, you blockheaded buffoon!"

Ricky rubbed his ruby-red cheek. "Ouch! What was *that* for? There's no need to be jealous just because..."

SLAP!

Emily whacked his other cheek. "Can't you ever just shut *up*. Listen to me! I've found proof that your new BFF, Mr. Perfect Painter, is a horrible killing machine. He murdered a man named Fredrick Flaymore. Last night I found Mr. Flaymore's grave in The Painter's backyard with a large X marked beside it. Crossed off The Painter's hit list. A list I'm positive *we're* on, too!"

Ricky chuckled. "You're always so uptight. The Painter

is obviously playing with a few cards short of a full deck, if you know what I mean, but he's also one of the nicest men I've ever known. Do you have actual proof that he murdered this Flaymore guy?"

Emily flushed. "Well, not *exactly*. The murder suspect was never caught. But the victim is buried in The Painter's back yard! How much more evidence do you need?" Her face was glowing red with frustration. "Ricky, sometimes you can be such an imbecile. You make me want to wring your scrawny little..." She paused. "Ricky? Are you even listening to me?"

All the color in Ricky's face had drained away and he was staring at the sky with glazed eyes. Emily followed his sight path but saw nothing unusual. "What's the matter?"

Ricky massaged his eyelids and pointed. "What's *that?*"

Emily shrugged. "Just a constellation of stars. You know, like the Big Dipper and Orion's Belt. Seriously dude, are you *sure* you're okay? You've seen that constellation like a thousand times before."

Ricky shook his head. "No, I haven't. I've only seen it once."

"What are you talking about?" She gave him a suspicious look. "It's been your favorite set of stars since we were kids. We called it *Mr. Muscles* because it looks like a weightlifter with massive biceps."

Ricky gulped. "I think we have a *big* problem."

The World According To Ricky

Ricky's brain felt like a clump of mashed potatoes with too much gravy. *You're overreacting*. Yet, no matter how hard he tried, he couldn't deny what he saw. The constellation of stars was *identical* to the one he had painted during their first lesson. *But that would mean....*

"Emily, you have to answer an important question."

Her eyebrows slanted. "Um, okay? Is something wrong?"

"It doesn't matter right now. Tell me, have we ever been to Mars?"

She gaped at him, unsure if this was a prank or if he had finally lost his mind. "Excuse me?"

"Just answer the question."

Emily laughed. "Of course not. That's completely

ridiculous!"

Ricky exhaled, relief swelling up inside him. *Thank goodness.* His fear was crazy after all. The stars were just that—*stars*. Nothing more.

"And I'm afraid we'll *never* go to Mars," Emily said. "Not after what happened last time."

Apparently Ricky's panic had not gone far, as it now came storming back with the force of a desperate cavalry charge. "*Last time?* What do you mean?"

"Are you serious?" Emily eyeballed him suspiciously. "Don't you *ever* pay attention in science class? We learned about this just last week."

"But you said we've *never* been to Mars."

"*We* haven't." She motioned between them. "As in *you and I*. But astronauts went there several years ago. Seriously, do you not remember *any* of this?"

"Just tell me," Ricky pressed. "What happened?"

"Well," Emily said, speaking slowly as if he had only learned English yesterday. "The spaceship landed on Mars. The spacemen even captured photographs of what looks like extraterrestrial life. Strange creatures with two heads and three wings."

A lump the size of a pear formed in Ricky's throat. "What happened to them? The astronauts, I mean."

"They died."

"How?"

Emily shrugged. "Something about a spaceship malfunction. I think the spaceship door became unhatched so they suffocated. Seriously, what is all this about?"

Ricky couldn't breathe. "This isn't good."

Ricky burst through the front door of his house. "James! Catherine!"

There was no answer.

Emily entered behind him. "Can you *please* explain what's wrong?"

Ricky pointed to the living room wall. Two boat oars were hung crisscrossed and a sea-captain hat was pinned above where the two oars met, forming the shape of a skull and crossbones. "Has this always been here?"

"Yeah, your mom hung that up there years ago."

"Where did it come from?"

"You inherited them from your grandpa Henry. He was a sailor before he became a preacher, but you've always insisted he was actually a pirate. Crazy, right?"

"Hey, dude, whaz' up?" said a voice behind him. Ricky turned—and screamed. James stood in the doorway wearing a far-too-tight T-shirt displaying some obscure punk band's logo. His long hair hung around him in a bob, except for the back, which was pulled into a greasy ponytail. He gave a head nod, causing the long bangs to flick. “What's wrong, bro?”

“Oh no-no-no.” Ricky ran for the stairs, clearing four steps at a time.

Emily called after him. “Where are you going?” Ricky ignored her. He dashed down the hall to his sister's bedroom. The Lego booby-traps that always fortified her room were nowhere to be seen.

“Catherine!” He threw the door open. Inside was a lone table with a sewing machine on top. Several shelves, filled with various containers of yarn and ribbon, were pressed against the walls. Ricky backed out of the door, pressing his hands to his forehead. "No-no-no!”

Emily and James stood in the hallway, both staring at him with concern. “Dude, what are you doing in mom's craft room?”

Sweat poured down Ricky's face. “Where is she? *WHERE IS SHE?*”

“Who? Mom?”

Ricky shook his head. “No. Where's *Catherine*?”

James and Emily exchanged looks. “Who is Catherine?”

“Our sister!” Ricky's eyes drifted to the framed family portraits on the wall. In every one was his mother and father, James, and himself. Occasionally, Chevy made an appearance as well. That was all. Ricky pulled the church directory photograph from his pocket. In it, he and James stood with arms over each other's shoulders. A full-length mirror was visible in the background. There was no sign of Catherine.

Emily placed a hand on Ricky's shoulder. "You *don't have* a sister."

A Rather Humongous Problem

Panic.

Hyperventilate.

Panic again.

Cover mouth to prevent upchucking.

Panic once more.

Repeat.

Ricky went through the process several times. Emily and James had dragged his dead-weight body to his bedroom and propped him against the bed. Emily sat before him, twiddling her thumbs. "You do realize everything you've told us sounds *completely insane*, right?"

Ricky nodded, unable to speak. James stroked his greasy long hair. "I wasn't supposed to tell you this, little bro, but when we were kids dad used to toss us into the air and catch us. Well, this one time he missed you, and..."

"*Anyways,*" Emily said, shooting James a stern look. "Ricky, you're saying that by *painting a picture* you changed history and erased your little sister? What did you say her name was again?"

"Catherine, but I called her Cat," Ricky whispered.

"And you also changed *the stars*? I have a hard time wrapping my head around that."

Ricky looked her straight in the eye. "You also had trouble believing The Painter was a bad guy at first."

"Good point," she admitted.

James wasn't so easily convinced. "I trust you, Ricky. If you say a painting changed the very fabric of world history then I'll dig it." He yanked on his ponytail. "What I *can't* accept is that I had *spiked* hair! What kind of wannabe rockstar would spike his hair like a porcupine?"

Ricky managed a grin. "I've been preaching that sermon for years."

Emily clapped her hands together. "Okay, let's just say that everything Ricky says is true." Her tone suggested that she *did not* think so. "We *do* know this Painter creep is a murderer. So what do we do about it?"

James was still preoccupied with his flowing locks, so Ricky answered. "We need to get him to change everything back." As irritating as Catherine had always been, now that she was gone he realized how much he would miss having her around (to torment, obviously).

Emily nodded. "Agreed. We need to trap him somehow. Force him to do what we want. We need a plan."

"We don't have much time," Ricky said. "He's expecting me back tomorrow night to finish his masterpiece. If I don't show up, he might suspect something is wrong. If he realizes that we know his secret, he might remove *us* from existence, too." Ricky sighed. He felt like they were trying to walk a chubby elephant across a bridge made of damp tissue paper.

"There's still one thing that doesn't make sense," Emily said, then frowned. "Okay, there are *a trillion* things that don't make sense. But why has The Painter gone through all this trouble to give you lessons? I mean, if he has the power to change the world through his paintings, why does he need *you*?"

Ricky wasn't sure if he should take offense at the comment. "It's almost as if he can't complete the masterwork alone. He said he's been working on it for years but can't finish it. What if he's been training me to finish it for him?"

"Maybe," Emily said slowly, the gears in her brain moving at full throttle. "We're running out of time to put this puzzle together. Tomorrow morning we will prepare." The fierce determination in her voice caused even James to regain his focus.

"And then what?"

Emily gazed out the window in the direction of Hallow's Drive. "And then hope we've done enough to avoid being killed."

Today's Forecast: Cloudy With a Chance of Death

How were you supposed to spend your last day before being murdered? Having never dealt with this particular predicament, Ricky was at a loss as to what to do. Emily had told them to prepare, but hadn't expounded on *what*, if anything, she actually had in mind.

Ricky decided he should get his soul in order before departing to the afterlife. He accompanied his parents to Sunday morning church. While sitting in the pew, Ricky compiled a lengthy list of sins to confess—the majority of which included awful (but really quite clever) pranks he'd played on his siblings over the years. He wondered if Catherine's removal from history meant he was no longer guilty of that portion of his transgressions.

As the preacher spoke on the book of Genesis about the creation of the world, Ricky let his mind wander. He thought of all the things he'd never experience due to his tragically shortened life. At the conclusion of the service, the preacher asked the congregation to bow in prayer. Ricky squeezed his hands together. "Well, God, I guess I'll be seeing you soon."

Ricky, James, and Emily gathered in the church playground after the service. They formed a huddle. "We need a plan of attack," James said, taking the lead.

"Agreed," Emily said. "I'll stop by Mumzy's Teashop. That's where Fredrick Flaymore was murdered. Maybe I'll uncover something useful."

"Good idea." James slapped Ricky on the back. "We'll go to the store and get some weapons and armor and stuff."

"Boys will be boys," Emily muttered, but agreed it wasn't a bad idea. "We'll meet back at your place in two hours. Good luck."

Ricky gulped. "We're gonna need it."

The fragrance of a thousand tea leaves engulfed Emily as she entered *Mumzy's Teashop*. On this day, not even the pleasant smell could soothe her jittery nerves. She looked around the same small store where a man had been murdered. For all she knew, Fredrick Flaymore had bled to death on the very spot where she now stood. The thought gave her chills.

A hand grabbed her shoulder.

Emily shrieked.

She spun and came face-to-face with an elderly lady. "I'm sorry, sweetie. Didn't mean to startle you."

"It's not your fault," Emily said quickly. "I'm just on edge today."

Mumzy patted her softly on the head. "Then you've come to the right place! I happen to have a two-for-one special on some nice soothing teas. Let me whip some up. *My treat.*"

Emily shook her head. "No, thank you. I'm here for a different reason."

Mumzy raised a penciled-on eyebrow. "You came to a teashop for something other than tea?"

"I was hoping to ask you a few questions, if that's alright."

"Of course, dearie," Mumzy said with a tender smile. "Ask away."

Emily dropped her gaze, tracing circles on the floor with her foot. "Do you know anything about the murder that took place here?"

Mumzy's artificial eyebrows seemed to leap right off her

face. “Good heavens! Why in the name of my mother’s furry earlobes do you want to know about *that* horrible incident?”

Emily looked up eagerly. “So you *do* know something about it?”

Mumzy nodded. “Not much, mind you, but some. The murder happened well before my time. Many years ago. My great grandma Jeanie owned the shop back then. Dreadful night! The awful experience haunted my great grandma for the rest of her life. Even on her deathbed, her last words were about that night. She whispered that she wished she had a second chance. But don’t ask me what she meant, because only the good Lord knows.”

“Did she know Fredrick Flaymore? Or why he was in the teashop that night? Or why he was murdered? Or who did it? Or...”

Mumzy raised her hands, chuckling. “Easy now, dearie. You’re *full* of questions!” She massaged her forehead, closing her eyes to concentrate. “If I remember correctly, Mr. Flaymore was a bit of a hermit. The type that kept to himself and didn’t bother anyone. Not the sort of man you’d expect to be murdered.” She sighed. “Such a shame, too. I’ve been told he was quite the talented artist.”

“He was an artist?”

“A prodigy, if the stories are true,” Mumzy said.

Was that the key? Had The Painter and Fredrick

Flaymore been bitter rivals? Did The Painter kill Flaymore to ensure that *he* was the best artist? Perhaps both sought to woo Mumzy's great grandmother with their talent? An idea suddenly popped into Emily's head.

"Are there any pictures from that night?"

The elderly woman frowned. "Well, yes. I have one of the police photographs stored in my archives. A ghastly thing to look at though."

"Can I please see it?"

Mumzy hesitated for moment, then sighed. "I suppose so, if only to quench your morbid curiosity. Give me a second to go fetch it." She disappeared through the back door.

Emily waited anxiously. The pieces of the puzzle were finally coming together. If she could uncover *why* The Painter had killed Mr. Flaymore then maybe she could figure out his current plan. Mumzy returned a few minutes later holding the photograph. Emily snatched it from her hand.

The black and white picture depicted the teashop which looked nearly identical to how it did now. The body of Fredrick Flaymore lay in the middle of the floor, arms and legs crumpled against his body like a dead, upside-down spider. A dark stain marked the middle of his chest below his bow tie. Beside the body was a single paintbrush. Emily concluded that the liquid oozing from the brush was *not* paint. She scrunched her face. There was something hauntingly familiar about the scene.

She gasped.

"Heavens! Are you alright?" Mumzy asked.

Emily swallowed, struggling to force the words out. "I think I'll take that calming tea after all." It wasn't the scene that was familiar. It was the *person.* She *recognized* Fredrick Flaymore. Despite the man's youth, there was no mistaking his rough facial features—it was The Painter.

A Picture of a Dead Person is Worth 1000 Words

"That's impossible!" Ricky said, looking across the circle at Emily and James. Piled on the floor between them were their newly purchased supplies, including, but not limited to, a bottle of pepper spray, a Nerf gun (with rapid-pump action), a yellow floatation vest, a noise-making toy helicopter, a badminton racket, and two jumbo-sized jars of soothing tea. The source of Ricky's alarm, however, was the small black and white photograph.

“He’s right,” James said. “The numbers don’t line up. If this Fredrick Flaymore guy was middle-aged when he was killed, and that was like a hundred years ago, then that would make The Painter...well... *really old.*” (Math was not James’ strong subject.)

"Not to mention *dead,*" Ricky added.

“But *look,*” Emily insisted, pointing to the victim’s face. “It looks *exactly* like him, or at least a younger version of him. It’s way too bizarre to be a coincidence.”

James' eyes lit up. "What if he's now an undead zombie raised to life by an evil wizard?"

"James, you're an idiot," Ricky said. "More likely its like his great, great ancestor. Or maybe the two men just look a lot alike. Kind of like me and Hercules."

"More like you and Jabba the Hutt," Emily whispered under her breath.

Ricky shot her suspicious glare, but she proceeded to look at the walls and ceiling as if she hadn't spoken a word all evening.

“None of this matters," James said. "Whoever the dead man in the picture is, The Painter *we* know is still *very much alive* and is still going to kill us tonight unless we come up with a plan to stop him.” His ominous words seemed to float to the ceiling, cluttering into a dark cloud above them. In unison, the trio pulled up their sleeves and checked their watches.

6:32 p.m.

They were running out of time. Further complicating matters, they still lacked anything with even a fleeting resemblance to a good plan. Emily scanned their sparse (and completely useless) inventory of supplies and grimaced. Why had she ever allowed two boys to handle the shopping? *This settles it. We're all going to die.*

"The key is to keep The Painter from realizing we're on to him," James said, repeating what they'd already concluded.

Emily looked to Ricky. "You need to go to your painting lesson and act as though there's nothing out of the ordinary."

"And by *nothing out of the ordinary,"* Ricky said, "I assume you mean the fact that my instructor is a raging killer who could blot me out of existence at any moment with a single stroke of his paintbrush?"

Emily nodded. "Yeah, something like that."

"Okay, just clarifying. No biggie, right?"

"Just stall as long as you can," James said. "You're the best one I know for such a task. Just pretend the painting is your math homework! Only, instead of algebra you might actually be dooming the world as we know it..." His voice trailed off. The pep-talk had sounded better in his head.

"James is right," Emily said, attempting to salvage the

pitiful remains of Ricky's courage. "While you distract The Painter, James and I will sneak in through the back door. Once inside, we'll try to break into that locked metal door. He's obviously hiding *something* in there. With any luck we'll find a way to defeat him."

"What if you *don't* find anything behind that door? I can't stall him forever." Ricky said.

"Then we'll take him by force." The fiery determination in Emily's voice was scary. "He may be a killer, but he's still just one old man. If we can catch him by surprise we might be able to overwhelm him by power of numbers."

"What about Van Gogh?" Ricky asked.

"The puppy?" Emily shook her head. "Unless you're worried about being licked to death, I don't think he'll be a problem."

Silence descended on them, as they let their imaginations drift down gloomy roads. Emily pulled her ponytail into her mouth and nervously chewed on it. James did likewise.

Beep! Beep! Beep!

The sound cut through the silence.

Ricky lunged onto Emily' lap, wrapping his arms around her neck. She huffed once more as James lunged onto *Ricky's* lap, wrapping his arms around *his* neck. "What was that!?"

Emily shoved the two boys off. "Chill out, you wimps. It's just my alarm." She looked at her watch. **7:00 p.m.** "Time to go."

They all nodded, but no one made the first move to stand. They stared at each other, waiting for someone to find enough bravery to take the lead. Then, to the surprise of all—*including James*—James stood. "Come! We have work to do! Onward! What's the worst that could happen?"

"We could all die," Ricky and Emily said together.

"Oh, yeah," James muttered. "I guess there's that."

He sat back down.

The Painter's beady eyes gazed at the large canvas before him.

His *masterwork.*

His *magnum opus.*

His *legacy.*

After so many long years he would finally achieve his goal. Tonight the world would change forever. He stroked his hand down Van Gogh's snout. *All was going according to plan.* The Painter turned and exited the room, closing the metal door behind him and fastening the three locks.

The time was near.

When Plan B Is As Lousy as Plan A

Patter…patter…patter…

Patter…patter…patter…

Patter…patter…patter…

Ricky, James, and Emily trekked slowly down the street, guided only by the weak light of their flashlight. The waning moon was blotched out by thick gray clouds and the streetlights flickered like dying strobe lamps.

No breeze blew.

No critters scurried.

No noise of any sort resounded in the night air.

A lone sliver of pallid light trickled out from behind the tattered window blinds of the Hallow's Drive mansion—The Painter was waiting for them.

Only James' chattering teeth broke the silence. His skin

had the appearance of snake-hide with a goosebumps infection. Ricky was in no place to judge. Every one of his fingers was bleeding from where he had pillaged his fingernails.

"Ricky," Emily whispered, once again chewing her ponytail like a piece of overcooked corn-on-the-cob. "I don't think you should be the one wearing the inflatable life vest. It's too obvious beneath your shirt. The Painter will notice."

Ricky flushed. "Um, actually, James is wearing the vest."

Emily's face reddened. "Oh...well...um...that's good then." She dropped her gaze. They had divided the supplies. James had claimed the Nerf Gun, the pepper-spray and, apparently, also the armor. Ricky had taken the noise-making helicopter to use as an alarm, should anything go askew. That left her with the badminton racket (the Cavanaugh brothers had obviously never witnessed her abysmal performances in gym class).

"You'll do great, Ricky," Emily said.

He tilted his head. "Then why do you keep staring at me like you'll never see me again?"

"Best to be prepared for any outcome," she said curtly, then gave him another sorrowful peek.

James took several steps then turned to face them. "We need more optimism here! Miracles have happened before.

Take Ricky, for example. The deck was stacked against him, but he passed *all of his* 4th grade exams."

"After taking fourth-grade twice," Emily noted.

"Exactly!" James bellowed. "Improvement! All we need is belief. It's like in all the great underdog movies. Nobody thought Rocky Balboa could win the boxing match against Apollo Creed, but he kept his head high and believed in himself!"

Ricky groaned. "Doesn't Rocky *lose* the match at the end of that movie?"

James' face fell. "Oh, yeah. I forgot." He fidgeted with his fingers. "Does he win in the sequel?"

Emily pushed him aside. "No offense, but that was the worst pep talk I've ever heard. I grow more and more discouraged every time you open your mouth." She sighed. "Let's just go do what we must and try not to get killed."

"Exactly!" James exclaimed, as though her interruption had been a rehearsed part of his clever speech.

"Turn the flashlight off," Emily said as they approached the house. "The Painter can't know James and I are here." With a *click* the street was plunged into total darkness.

Ricky stared through the black iron gate at the ominous manor—the house of a murderer. A house that would likely be the location of his own untimely (and less-than-pleasant) death. He glanced to Emily and James (who looked like a walking marshmallow with the life vest beneath his hoodie). James appeared wobbly, clearly on the verge of fainting. Emily wasn't faring much better. She gave Ricky a feeble wave.

With a final breath, Ricky marched up to the door and knocked three times. The door slowly opened. "Please come in." The Painter's words slithered from his mouth like a snake's hiss. "Today is a special day. We haven't a moment to lose."

Ricky looked over his shoulder, back into the night. There was no sign of James or Emily. They had already gone to carry out their task. He needed to stay focused on *his* task. He stepped into the house. As he did, a strange scent entered his nostrils. Not the usual aroma of tea. Something stronger. Something stale. Something *unpleasant*. A lump grew in Ricky's throat. He recognized the smell. It was the smell of blood.

From Bad to Worse to Utterly Disastrous

Blood.

There was no mistaking the stench. It was not fresh, like a newly acquired knee scrape or paper cut. It smelled old and stale, like a long-forgotten Band-Aid. Ricky gagged, wondering whose blood was serving as the evening's potpourri. Unless he was careful, he knew *his* blood would be contributing to the fragrance before the night was over.

Ricky walked as if his legs had been marinated in molasses overnight; dragging his feet forward without the soles of his sandals ever leaving the ground. *Delay at all costs.* That was his only duty. To buy James and Emily time to do...well, whatever it was they were going to do (their plan had been rather sparse on details).

Up ahead, The Painter moved down the hall with remarkable velocity for a hunch-backed man with a cane. He was not his usual jabbering self. Not even a single tea-related comment passed between his yellow-stained teeth. In fact, he didn't appear to even realize that Ricky had fallen behind.

As if reading Ricky's thoughts, The Painter came to an abrupt stop. He cranked his neck, his pointed chin hooking over his shoulder and his eyes pinning on Ricky.

"Is there a problem, young man?"

Ricky gulped, bumbling, "Um...no...of course not...I mean..."

Whoosh.

In the blink of the eye The Painter stood towering over him, peering down like a lion who had just stumbled across a sleeping gazelle. Ricky was about to spout the first lie that came to mind, that he needed to tie his shoes, but caught himself. He wouldn't make the same silly mistake twice. Instead, he said, "I was just admiring your beautiful paintings. I've never seen anything even *half* as lovely!"

The Painter didn't blink.

Ricky looked to the wall-sized painting beside him, a portrait of the most hideous woman he had ever seen. There were more fuzzy warts on her face than strands of hair on her head, at least seven overlapping chins, and a nose so long several pigeons could perch quite comfortably upon it. "I'm sure she had a beautiful soul," he muttered.

"Indeed." The Painter said without inflection. "Shall we continue?" Ricky nodded silently, not trusting his tongue to avoid another stupid blunder. The Painter extended a hand. "Lead the way." Without another choice, Ricky proceeded down the long hallway. As they reached the metal door The Painter cleared his throat. "Excuse me while I grab the paint." He unlocked the three deadbolts and pulled the door open.

The instant he did, a putrid odor flooded out. The stink was nauseating. There was no doubt, Ricky had discovered the origin of the stale-smelling blood. The Painter slipped inside and pulled the door closed behind him. Ricky wondered how James and Emily were faring. He found slight comfort in knowing that they couldn't be doing any *worse*.

The *click* of the opening door caused Ricky to jump. The Painter reappeared in the doorframe, a palette of colorful paint in his hand. He gave Ricky a quizzical stare. "You're acting quite peculiar tonight."

"I'm just *so excited* to start painting," Ricky said quickly. "And for some of that wonderful tea." The words struck the bull's-eye. The Painter's face lit up like a Christmas tree.

"*Drats!* I forgot about the tea! It's probably getting cold by now!" He darted down the hall to rescue the cooling tea, letting the metal door slide slowly closed behind him.

Ricky shot a quick glance to The Painter, then back to the door. There was no time for second-guessing. He flicked his foot, launching a sandal toward the door. It lodged into the crack just in time to stop the door from fully closing.

He grinned, impressed with himself. Perhaps the evening wouldn't be as disastrous as they had thought. When he reached the now-familiar room at the back of the house, The Painter was waiting. The moonlight reflected off his coarse skin, giving him a spectral appearance.

The sight made Ricky pause. *Wait a second, where's the moonlight coming from?* His newfound hope died a quick and agonizing death as he discovered the answer. The entire wall was one large window that offered a full view to the graveyard.

Had the window always been there? Ricky was positive that there had not been any windows whatsoever on the back of the house. Yet, at the same time, somehow he couldn't remember the large window having ever *not* been there. The memory was like a dream that was rapidly fading away from recollection.

Two faint shadows were moving in the back yard below. The Painter stood gazing out the window with his hands clasped behind his back. Ricky's skin went ice cold with the terrible realization that James and Emily were about to unknowingly walk straight into The Painter's view. If they were seen, everything—including their lives—was over.

A High Stakes Game of Hide-and-Seek

James was no coward. He reminded himself of this over and over as he inched forward, trailing several feet behind Emily. His all-consuming phobia of spiders was, after all, completely justified. After all, no one would dare call a man a coward for being too afraid to tightrope walk over a lake of seething lava—and lakes of seething lava didn't even have hairy legs! No, James was no coward.

Emily pointed toward a large tree. "*Pssst.* Look." A man of lesser courage would have felt uneasy about the skeletal tree, but not James (although the leafless branches *did* have the unsightly appearance of insect legs).

He had to keep his cool for Emily's sake. As a *man*, he needed to be a gallant anchor of unshakable bravery for the faint-hearted damsel. He glanced down the tree trunk and spotted something else. Claw marks carved deep into the bark.

In that moment, James had a beautiful epiphany—there was absolutely nothing shameful about being a coward. Satisfied with his new resolution, he bellowed an ear-piercing shriek.

Emily's swatted the back of his head. "*Shush, you sissy!*" Before James could unleash another primal scream, a gigantic vulture swooped over their heads and landed on one of the tree's branches. The limb sagged under the beast's weight as the dinosaur-sized menace eyed them with what James could only interpret as a "hungry" stare.

Dust flew as James bolted away from the tree toward the back yard, arms flailing above his head like soggy noodles. He was too terror stricken to even remember the discovery of his cowardice. Otherwise, he would have thought to retreat in the opposite direction, back to the safety of the street. By the time he realized the error it was already too late. Sprawling out before him as far as he could see was the foggy graveyard.

Emily yanked him backwards and pointed toward the house. A huge window covered most of the wall. Perched dead-center behind the glass, like a gargoyle peering down from the walls of an ancient castle, was The Painter. His scrutinizing gaze slowly turned in their direction.

There was no time to think. Ricky acted upon the first thought that popped into his mind—and began to sing. "The ants go marching one by one, hurrah, hurrah! The ants go marching..."

The Painter twirled around, a stunned expression plastered on his face. His eyes drifted to the half-empty cup of tea in Ricky's hand, likely wondering if the tea had been accidentally swapped out for strong booze. Over The Painter's shoulder Ricky saw James run into view. The Painter spun back around.

Emily grabbed James and tugged him down into the fog and out of view just in time. Ricky grimaced. They had narrowly dodged a bullet. Clearly, matters were going to be far more complicated than they had anticipated.

The Painter continued to survey the back yard. *He senses that something is up.* Ricky needed to divert his attention again. "This tea is making me feel funky." He shook his cup. "And it's *cold*! Didn't you say an artist couldn't paint unless the tea was *just right*?"

The Painter turned. "I suppose I did say that, didn't I?" Behind him, James and Emily reappeared into view and frantically scrambled across the yard. Ricky was so distracted by the sight that he didn't even notice The Painter approach and take his teacup. The old man's eyes widened as his fingers felt the scathing heat from Ricky's *not-as-cold-as-advertised* cup.

"If you'll excuse me," The Painter said in a slow drone. "I'll fetch you some fresh tea. I keep the tea-leaves in the hallway room." The master artist hastened toward the exit. Ricky's sigh of relief stopped abruptly when the implications of the words registered: he would discover the flip-flop jamming the metal door.

"I don't want tea!" Ricky blurted, diving to block the exit.

The Painter waved him off. "*Nonsense*. It will only take a moment." He stepped around Ricky and departed down the hall.

"NO! I'm allergic to tea! It gives me gas!"

The Painter turned, his face aghast. "*Oh!* Why didn't you say so before?"

"Well...I...you see...it's just..." Ricky's lips flapped, struggling to form a response.

The Painter sighed and reentered the room. "Very well, no tea." Outside, James and Emily dropped back to the ground, now stranded in the middle of the yard. They would be easily spotted by a focused eye. Ricky couldn't allow that to happen.

"So," Ricky began, stepping forward to place himself between The Painter's sightline and the window. "Tell me about this great masterpiece we're finishing tonight." He took the elder man by the arm and guided him to the center of the room where a single canvas was displayed.

The huge canvas, roughly the size of a refrigerator set sideways, was entirely concealed under a purple tarp. All except for one small opening where a square of fabric had been cut out to reveal the white canvas behind.

"What is it?" Ricky asked.

"That's not important," The Painter said. "All that matters is what it *will* be." He motioned toward the exposed square. "Shall we begin?"

Out of the corner of his eye, Ricky saw the blurry silhouettes of James and Emily streaking by. *Hurry up, guys.* He cracked his knuckles. "Okay. Let's do it."

Divide and ~~Conquer~~ Die

If Emily held her breath for much longer she worried she'd forget *how* to breathe. Her face had morphed into a plum with eyes and her head felt ready to burst. Ricky had convinced The Painter to leave the room only to call him back seconds later. *What on earth are you doing, Ricky?*

James crouched beside her, his face a bright shade of orange-ish turquoise. Biology wasn't Emily's strongest subject, but she knew enough to deduce that such skin color was neither natural nor healthy. Fortunately, Ricky *finally* led The Painter away from the window.

A forceful wind blew across the back yard—or at least that's how it felt when James finally exhaled. He clawed at this throat and gasped for breath. "I thought I was going to explode!"

"Quick," Emily said, motioning to the large window. "I

don't know how much longer Ricky can distract The Painter." They started to rush toward the back door—only to discover that *there wasn't one*. They stopped dead in their tracks. Emily couldn't believe they had made such a glaring oversight. They had been certain there was a rear entrance. *Unless...*

If The Painter had the power to wipe out *a person*, then surely he could erase a door. Emily rubbed her eyes. If her hypothesis were true, then The Painter had altered his house to keep them out. That meant he knew they were coming. If so, they were in even more danger than they thought.

They didn't dare try the front door with yappy Van Gogh inside, but, with no back door, their only option was the graveyard. Unless The Painter had thought to remove the trapdoors as well, they might still be able to sneak into the house unnoticed. The only question was—how to find one?

She and James crawled on all fours, patting the ground in search of the secret entrances. These trapdoors were like pennies—always getting in the way and then disappearing when you actually needed one. Their search continued for several more fruitless minutes.

"We're running out of time," Emily groaned. She stood and scanned the graveyard. The ever-present carpet of fog made it impossible to see anything.

"Emily! Down!" James hissed.

The Painter had turned once again to look outside.

Emily dove forward to hide behind one of the tombstones. She crashed into the ground...and kept falling. The ground beneath her gave out, spinning like a revolving door, and she plunged a dozen feet straight down.

CRASH!

"Umph!"

Emily smashed face-first onto a sand-covered floor. She released a pained moan, wishing *she* had been wearing the inflatable life vest. There were several *clicks* and *pops* as the mechanical trapdoor fixed back into place.

James' muffled voice called from the other side. "Emily! Are you okay?"

"I think so," she said, touching her throbbing nose and discovering that it was bleeding. She had fallen into a small cellar. At the other end of a lone corridor was a wooden ladder. "And I may have found a way into the house. Get down here."

There were several muted *bangs* from above, and then James' breathy voice. "I can't. The trapdoor won't budge!"

"There has to be another one somewhere. Just keep looking."

"What about you?"

She turned to the passageway. "I'll go on alone. If I can get inside, maybe I can let you through the front door."

There was no response.

"James?"

Silence.

Something must have spooked him. Nothing I can do about it down here. She dusted the sand from her clothes. *Here goes nothing.* She began the long march down the dark catacomb, knowing that no matter how terrified she was now, whatever waited on the other end was bound to be much, *much* worse.

Big Fluffy Terrors

Ricky pretended to listen to The Painter's instructions. His *true* focus was over his teacher's shoulder and out the window behind him. Ricky had seen both Emily and James dive for cover—but only James had stood back up.

He felt a flicker of relief when he finally saw another shape moving in the shadows. That hope was short-lived. The shape was much too large to be Emily. Ricky chomped down on his tongue. He wanted to scream a warning but knew James wouldn't hear him. He could do nothing but watch as the monstrous shape stalked toward James like a jaguar on the prowl.

Something stirred in the shadows. James ducked

behind a tombstone, peering into the gloom. He waited a full minute but saw no trace of anything sinister lurking in the mist. *I'm jumping at shadows.* He abandoned the hiding spot and resumed his search for a second trapdoor.

Snap.

James spun and raised his fists into a fighting stance—but there was nothing behind him. Keeping his fists up, he ventured farther into the graveyard, his body trembling from his toes to his eyebrows.

SNAP!

He whirled around again, tossing a blind punch into the fog.

Nothing.

He walked backwards, swiveling his head left and right. Something cold and hard pressed against his back. He twirled and threw another punch.

SMACK!

"*Ouch!*"

James shook his fist and examined the grave marker that had ambushed him. He read the inscription on the stone—and a sick feeling swelled in his stomach. He moved to the next tombstone and read the engraving. The sensation in his belly burned hotter. He continued to the next tombstone in the line, and then the next. Each stone confirmed his worst suspicion. *This is not good. This is not good at all.* He needed to warn Ricky and Emily about his discovery before it was too late.

SNAP!

He spun around.

This time there *was* something there.

James shrieked, but his panic morphed into relieved chuckles. The *deadly creature* of his imagination was no more than the little fluff-ball puppy, Van Gogh. The adorable mutt wagged her tail and vigorously licked his shoe.

"You scared me half to death," James whispered, patting the dog on the head. He straightened and turned to leave—only to come face-to-face with a monstrous beast the size of bloated hippo.

James' blood went ice cold. Ricky had spoken true—the creature's fangs *were* like samurai swords. Before James could even release a whimper, the monster pounced, and its razor teeth chomped down on his chest.

Breaking and Entering

The only thought that gave Emily the courage to press on down the narrow, musky corridor was Ricky. Not out of concern for his safety, mind you, but because she couldn't bear his obnoxious gloating at being brave enough to go in alone when she wasn't. She increased her pace. Some things were worse than death.

Emily reached the wooden ladder at the end of the passageway. Several of the rungs were splintered or missing altogether. *Think of Ricky gloating. Think of Ricky gloating. Think of Ricky gloating.* She grabbed the first rung and began her slow ascent.

The ladder wobbled unsteadily as she climbed.

SNAP!

A rung broke, sending Emily plummeting straight

down. She reached out and clasped another rung to break the fall. Her feet dangled as she hung on, suspended in the air. Regaining her footing, Emily resumed the climb. She reached the top without further incident. There was a square door on the ceiling. Undoing the latch, Emily pushed it open and pulled herself through it. She froze at what she saw on the other side.

This is not good.

In fact, it was the worst scenario imaginable.

Glancing out the window, Ricky could see no trace of James or Emily, nor of the enormous shape that had been creeping through the shadows. Ricky hoped their disappearance was a good sign—an indication that they had found a way into the house. The tide was turning at last.

Ricky didn't know anyone as resourceful as Emily. He had learned the hard way never to bet against her when she set her stubborn mind to a task. Most likely she was already inside the forbidden room, conjuring up a fail-proof plan to defeat The Painter. Ricky stretched an arm above his head and rotated his torso. He turned left and saw the abandoned graveyard outside. He turned right and saw...*Emily?*

She stood only a dozen feet behind him, bug-eyed and

motionless as if she'd been turned to stone. Ricky's own eyes bulged in surprise. He glanced to The Painter. The old artist was too busy chugging the last of his pre-painting tea to notice anything out of the ordinary. Ricky pretended to stretch his other arm and mouthed to Emily, *"Get out of here! Go to the metal door!"*

"I can't!" she mimed back, pointing to the wooden floor. Her meaning was clear. If she took another step the wood planks would creak. She frantically waved her hands at him. That gesture was equally clear: *DO SOMETHING!* Ricky scowled. *So typical.* It wasn't *his* fault that she had entered the massive house in the worst place possible. *Girls,* he thought with annoyance.

"Are you even listening to me?" The Painter asked. Ricky turned and met his teacher's level stare.

"Of course," Ricky lied. "You were just talking about...um...paint and tea...and stuff."

The Painter stroked his sharp chin. "Indeed." The temperature in the room seemed to drop by a dozen degrees at once, as if The Painter had breathed in all the room's warmth. If he turned around now, he'd easily spot Emily. Ricky had to do something—and *fast.*

He pressed a fist to his mouth. *Cough. Cough. COUGH! Cough.* "Ah, I'm choking on my own spit!" *COUGH. COUGH! Cough!* He hoped Emily was smart enough to take the hint and run.

The Painter slapped his back. "Deep breaths. Nice and slow." Ricky did as told, which turned out to be a bad idea. He gagged and the fake coughing fit was instantly silenced. In the absence of the noise, another sound was jarringly audible.

Creeak. Creeeeeak. Creak. Creeeeeak.

Emily halted, but not soon enough. The damage was done.

The Painter raised an eyebrow. "Van Gogh, is that you?" He turned his head toward the sound, to where Emily stood helpless in the dead center of the room.

Weeeeoooooeeee!

BWEEP bip bip BWEEP!

Weeeeeeeoooooooo WEEEEooooo!

Bweep!

"What in the name of Leonardo da Vinci's weak ankles is that *noise*?" The Painter exclaimed. Ricky held the toy helicopter, continuing to pound the buttons and produce a disjointed array of ear-splitting noise.

"I'm sorry, I don't know how to make it stop!" He continued hitting the buttons. *Run Emily!* he thought. The Painter snatched the helicopter out of his hands. After a few seconds the noises ceased. "Oh," Ricky said dumbly. "I guess if you just leave it alone it stops. Who knew?"

The Painter narrowed his eyes. He turned and scanned

the now-empty room behind him. "You scared poor Van Gogh away," he noted, with a hint of suspicion. "Now that we've gotten all our distractions out of the way, shall we finally begin?" The words carried an unmistakable threat.

Ricky glanced around the room and saw the tips of Emily's shoes protruding from behind a chair. She was hidden from sight, but was still trapped. Ricky was running out of ideas. "You sure you don't want some more tea first?"

"Oh, I've had my fill." All previous amusement was gone from The Painter's voice. Ricky had enough good sense to realize that he'd pushed his luck as far as he dared.

"Okay, just thought I'd check. Let's get started then."

The Painter tapped his long, skinny fingers together. "Splendid. This painting experience will be different than the others."

"What do you mean?" Ricky had a gut feeling that he wouldn't like the answer.

"Because this time I'm coming in with you. It is *my masterpiece* after all."

A lump formed in Ricky's throat. His gut had been right. "You can do that?"

The Painter nodded. "Of course. Collaboration is a long-standing tradition in art. Although a vastly overrated one, if you ask me."

"How does it work?"

"It's quite simple," The Painter said, speaking in the tone of a brilliant professor bored by the basics of his own subject. "I need only to touch your arm when you begin to paint and we will journey into the realm of creative possibility together. Only *you* will be able to create. *You're* the one wielding the brush, after all. But I will be able to interact with the creation and assist you in the process. I wouldn't dream of missing the completion of my masterpiece."

Ricky tried not to let the worry show on his face. It would be significantly harder to delay if The Painter was inside the painting with him. Ricky had the sickening feeling that The Painter knew this as well. "From the moment I first saw you outside my window I knew you were the one destined to help me achieve greatness."

The moment caught Ricky off guard. "Really? Because returning my ripped shirt *soaked in blood* was probably not the best invitation to partnership!"

The Painter chuckled. "Oh, yes, about that. I had intended to return your shirt as a token of goodwill, by using the painting portal to paint it on your doorstep, of course. Didn't you notice, I even fixed the rips. However, upon finishing I tripped over Van Gogh and spilled a splotch of red paint on the canvas. That little rascal is always causing problems." The old man flashed a toothy leer. "But enough chit-chat. Shall we begin?" He gripped Ricky's arm with his bony hand.

There was no going back.

Ricky dipped the brush in the paint. His heart raced as he pressed the bristles against the exposed canvas. The world started to spin.

From behind a tall chair, Emily watched in astonishment as both Ricky and The Painter's bodies went stiff and their eyes turned completely white. Neither appeared to even be breathing. Only Ricky's arm moved, stroking the brush across the canvas with such inhuman speed that his arm had become no more than blur. Meanwhile, the paint swirled on the canvas as though it had a mind of its own. The sight was hypnotizing.

Emily briefly considered knocking the petrified murderer over the head with the chair. The idea was tempting, but she wasn't sure how that might affect Ricky. Were he and The Painter connected somehow? Would Ricky be trapped inside the painting forever? The risk was far too great.

Exiting the room, she was immediately met with a foul smell. The farther down the hallway she ventured the stronger the stench became. She had to pinch her nose to keep from vomiting. Reaching the metal door, she spied Ricky's left flip-flop jammed in the crack, holding it open. *Perhaps he's not as useless as he seems.*

She pushed the door open. A flood of strong odors overtook her. Lavender. Mint. Chai. Jasmine. As well as an array of fruity fragrances. The strongest scent of all, however, by a large margin, was *blood.* Emily entered the room and gasped in horror at what she saw.

The More the Merrier

Hundreds of glass jars filled with blood. Floor-to-ceiling shelves displayed the sickening contents the way her grandma stored her favorite pickled okra. Emily looked away, unable to stand the sight. The Painter was even more devilish than she had imagined.

She wondered whose blood filled the jars. Was it harvested from the victims buried in the backyard? Would *she* contribute to The Painter's vile blood bank before the night was over? *You will if you keep standing around!* She pressed forward.

Along the other wall were more jars on shelves, although these containers only stored various tea leaves. Her feminine instinct thought the kitchen pantry would have been a better place to keep the tea, but she couldn't expect a man to possess that much common sense.

The narrow room seemed to stretch on for infinity, with the far end shrouded in shadow. Emily slowed to examine several framed paintings on the wall beside the shelves. Each was an identical self-portrait of The Painter. *That's odd.* Although she could imagine James decorating his room in a similar manner.

Emily reached the far end of the room and felt a sharp pang of disappointment. There was nothing there. Or at least, nothing useful to defeat The Painter. Only an empty easel (which must have held his masterpiece), a stack of extra canvases, and an assortment of other random painting material.

She stepped forward and heard something crunch beneath her feet. She bent and retrieved a crumpled piece of paper. Printed on it was a familiar image that Emily remembered studying in art class. It was the famous painting by Michelangelo called *The Creation of Adam.* The painting depicted God and Adam touching fingers, a representation of the moment when God had created the first man.

Emily flipped the paper over, seeking a clue as to its purpose, but found nothing. She let the picture flutter to the floor. Having come up empty, she needed to rescue Ricky and escape the haunted house. She turned to leave—just in time to see a body rushing toward her.

Emily screamed and unleashed a vicious kick to the assailant's belly.

"Umph!"

The attacker staggered backwards, gasping for wind. Emily looked closer. "*James!?* How did you get in here?" His clothes were shredded and the inflatable life jacket was deflated. "Oh my goodness, what happened to you!"

James rubbed his stomach. "*Van Gogh* happened to me."

"The cute little puppy did this to you?"

James shook his head, "*Heavens, no!* The gargantuan, bloodthirsty, teenage-boy-eating *monstrosity* did this to me! Had I not been wearing this life vest the creature's fangs would have ripped me to pieces! The only reason I'm *here* and not swimming in stomach fluids is because it tossed me right onto another trap door." He paused, leaning over to catch his breath. "The Painter has two pets after all. Gosh. Ricky was right."

Emily frowned in confusion (as she did whenever Ricky proved to be correct). "None of this makes sense."

A chilly voice sounded behind them. "Doesn't it?"

They spun to see The Painter filling the doorframe, and blocking their only exit. The lanky artist stood in the shadows like a menacing scarecrow guarding its turf with its unchanging, lifeless gaze.

"What have you done to Ricky?" Emily demanded. "You're supposed to be with him in the other room, inside the painting portal!"

The Painter sneered. "Oh, but I am."

"Huh?" Emily straightened her posture. "Don't waste our time with riddles. If you're going to kill us then what are you waiting for?"

The Painter raised an eyebrow. "*Kill* you? Why would you think that? Do you think I'm some kind of monster?"

"No, I think you're a *murderer*." Emily jabbed a finger at his chest. "Before you buried me alive you admitted to killing all the people in the graveyard. We know you killed Fredrick Flaymore!"

"Hmm, I suppose I did." The Painter motioned to the jars beside him. "Come to think of it, I have Mr. Flaymore's blood right here. A lovely keepsake, wouldn't you say?"

Emily scrunched her face in revulsion. James leaned in and whispered, "I need to tell you something,"

"Not now," she said.

"It's important. I found something in the graveyard."

The Painter appeared in no rush to exterminate them, so Emily sighed and turned to James. "*What?*"

"Remember the X you found on the tombstone after Fredrick Flaymore's name?"

She nodded. *How could she forget?* "The one The Painter added after crossing him off his murder hit list."

"No," James said. "Well, *maybe*. That's not the point. The point is that the X isn't a letter. It's a *number*."

Emily frowned. "A number? What are you talking about?"

"An X is the *Roman numeral* for the number ten." James hesitated, reluctant to continue. "I looked at the other graves. Every tombstone has a different Roman Numeral after the name."

"So what? I don't see your point."

"My point," James said. "Is that every grave has a different number, but they all have the *same name*—Fredrick Flaymore."

Emily looked back at the madman in the doorway. For the first time she noticed the dark scab marks lined across his colorless forehead. She thrust a finger toward him. "Those cuts weren't there when I tried to show Ricky. How is that possible? It's like..." her voice trailed off.

In the other room with Ricky The Painter's hair had hung loose to his shoulders, but now it was pulled into a familiar ponytail. She also noticed that The Painter was standing quite well without his cane. A fat lump dropped into her stomach. Her eyes drifted to the self-portraits hanging on the wall. In that instant everything made sense. The final piece of the jigsaw puzzle had been set in place, and the image it revealed was horrifying.

Emily's voice was no more than a hoarse whisper. "You painted yourself."

He nodded. "I did."

"But that would mean..."

The Painter smiled. "The more the merrier."

A Jealous Rival of Cosmic Proportions

The Painter's warm breath had the distinct smell of mango-mint tea as it tickled the back of Ricky's neck. As with the previous ventures into the painting portal, Ricky was floating in an expanse of white nothingness. *Unlike* those times, he could faintly perceive distant color on the fringe of his vision. The pigment likely belonged to The Painter's previous work on his masterpiece. Ricky strained his eyes for a better view.

"Don't look around you," The Painter said curtly. "What already exists is of no importance to you. Your only concern is that which has *not yet* been completed." The Painter circled in front of Ricky, obscuring his view of the distant color. "Are you ready?"

"What should I paint?"

The Painter tapped his chest above his heart. "Me."

"You?"

"Isn't that what I just said?" The Painter sounded annoyed. His hands were sweating with anticipation.

"I suppose so," Ricky said. "Couldn't you paint yourself? No one knows *you* better than *you*, right?"

The Painter's eyes twitched, a tint of madness glimmering in them. "Not necessarily. As with anything else, a person's perception of themselves is colored, so to speak, by their own thoughts. If I believed with all my heart that I had three eyeballs would that make it true, just because *I* thought so?"

"No, I guess not."

The Painter dried his clammy hands on his pants. "Enough chatter. We have a masterpiece to complete and a world to change!" He set his cane down and laid on his side. "Your depiction of me must be *exact*. Just as I am now. Do you understand?"

Ricky nodded.

"Good." The Painter stretched his arm and extended his pointer-finger toward the border of color. "Begin."

Emily looked at the scar-faced man with a mixture of

awe and horror (although a significantly bigger portion of the latter). "The murder victims—they're all *you.*" She struggled to wrap her mind around all the revelation's sick implications. "*You're* Fredrick Flaymore."

The Painter gave a graceful bow. "Humbly at your service."

"So all those people buried in the graveyard are *you*?"

"In a manner of speaking," The Painter said. "More specifically, they are a painted expression of myself."

James raised an eyebrow. "A painted *expres-a-huh*?"

"Like a clone," Emily said in quick explanation. "But why? It sounds awful! You continuously create yourself just to die over and over again? *Why*?"

The Painter answered without hesitation. "Immortality." He motioned to the self-portraits on the wall. "I paint a younger version of myself. My older self teaches the new me all the secrets of the painting portal. Then, eventually, I sacrifice myself in order to allow the younger me to carry on the mission."

"*The mission?*"

The Painter shrugged, as if the answer should have been self-evident to all but the biggest fools. "To become the greatest artist of all time."

"But surely you *are* the greatest," James said. "I mean, your creations *come to life*! Your art literally changes the world. No one can rival that."

The Painter's face darkened. "I once thought so as well."

"You've accomplished such amazing feats," Emily said. "Can't you be satisfied with that? Why is it so important to be *the best*? What reason is worth dying over and over and over for?"

"Love," he whispered.

"Huh?" said Emily and James together, completely caught off guard.

The Painter sighed. "Is it *so hard* to believe a decrepit old man like me was once in love? I was a young artist, a hopeless romantic, and lover of all beauty—in particular, an angel named Jeanie. A simple girl with a heart as golden as the fine hair on her head." He closed his eyes, savoring the memory. "She would sit and watch me paint all afternoon. Never saying a word. Just watching. Just being there. Comforting me. Those were moments that made me realize I wanted to spend the rest of my life with her."

Emily's face brightened. Even amidst a dreary situation, the thought of a wedding excited her. "You asked her to marry you?"

"No," he said. "First I asked permission from her father. He was a hard and intelligent man with high standards for himself and impossible standards for his only daughter."

"What did he say?"

A single tear rolled down The Painter's wrinkled cheek. "He asked what I had to offer her. I knew he wouldn't be easily impressed, so I showed him my most prized paintings. I told him that I was the greatest artist alive."

"And?"

"He said I was wrong." The brief tranquility that had settled over The Painter burned away in a boiling fury. "My offering wasn't enough. There was one artist even better, he claimed. An artist I could *never* hope to match in originality or skill. Until I accepted this truth, he refused to give me his blessing."

Emily wiped the moisture forming in her own eyes. "I'm so sorry. That must have been difficult to hear."

"Difficult?" The Painter released a joyless cackle. "It was *death*! My entire world came crashing down! I became more determined than ever. Driven to the brink of insanity to prove him wrong. It became my obsession. My *life*. But no matter what I did, I could never achieve the greatness of my new rival artist. Eventually I lost all hope and stabbed myself in the heart with my own paintbrush."

Emily covered her mouth, suffocating a gasp. "Inside Mumzy's teashop," she said, realization hitting her. "Jeanie was Mumzy's great grandmother. That's why you love tea so much. It reminds you of her."

The Painter nodded. "Yes, although that night I

discovered tea has more *functional* purposes as well."

"What do you mean?"

"As I bled to death, my last living act was one final attempt to achieve my goal. One final painting. With no paint, I used the only material available."

"Your blood," James said in a hoarse whisper.

"Flowing from my own heart." The Painter's lips curved into a slight grin, as though he found some sick amusement in the thought. "Short on time, I used the tea leaves to add colored pigment to my red blood. That night I entered the painting portal for the first time."

"That's why Ricky was able to enter into his paintings," Emily said. "You used the blood from the t-shirt he left behind."

The Painter nodded in affirmation. "My first time, in Jeanie's teashop, I didn't yet understand the full potential of blood-painting, as I now call it. Realizing I was about to die on the cusp of my monumental breakthrough, I painted myself. That night I watched myself die."

The Painter's lack of emotion was spine-chilling. "Fueled by newfound hope, I focused all my energy on outdoing my arch-rival at long last. The years passed slowly. At first I would wait for the older copy of myself to die of old age, but eventually I was forced to sacrifice myself faster in order to supply enough blood to keep up with my painting.

I discovered, however, that my first death had forever changed me. I no longer remembered the man I once was. The young, romantic artist who used to love nature's beauty was gone, never to return. As a result, I cannot paint a version of myself younger than the time of that first death. If a blood-painting is not *exact*, its transformative power will not work.

Despite my extraordinary new ability, I realized I was still only second best. I could change the world, but I couldn't create anything *new*. I can paint a flower, but only because a flower already exists outside my window. That is, until now." A devilish sneer molded on his face. "At this very moment the older version of me is with Ricky completing my masterwork. The achievement that will, at long last, prove *I* am the greatest creator alive."

James cleared his throat, the sound as feeble as a child's hiccup. "Who is this rival that you keep talking about?"

The Painter squeezed his fists until his knuckles turned white. "God."

"*God?*" Emily exclaimed, aghast. "You're competing with *God?*"

"Yes!" The Painter's face turned red. "No matter what I do, my art always pales in comparison to the originality of the mountains, the beauty of the stars, or the serenity of a calm moonlit lake. It's maddening! But soon everything will change."

In that moment, Emily came to a sickening realization. "That's what the picture on the floor was for. The painting by Michelangelo. The image of God creating man. *That's* your mission. You realized you could never beat God so you stopped trying to. Oh my gosh, *that's* your masterpiece. That's what you're having Ricky paint for you. He's going to paint you in the place of God. But if he does that, then..."

The Painter nodded. "Then I will *become* God."

Ricky studied The Painter's odd pose. *I can't delay any longer*. He concentrated. Color bubbled into existence, filling the white canvas, and slowly forming an outline of The Painter.

A Mountaintop Experience

Unless they stopped The Painter quickly, the world as they knew it would cease to exist. "Don't," Emily pleaded. "You don't realize what you're doing. It's not too late. You don't have to do this." Her body trembled as she groveled before the crazed artist. Her desperate petitions bounced harmlessly off The Painter like pebbles tossed against a brick wall.

His expression was one of genuine pity. "Oh, but I'm afraid I *must*. This is the only way to make things right. I've spent my entire life waiting for *this* very moment." He stretched his arms out, palms up. "Any second now I will no longer be forced to play second fiddle. I will become God!" He closed his eyes, sniffing the air and exhaling a satisfied sigh.

Emily whispered in James' ear. "Buy me a few minutes. I have an idea."

"*How*?"

Emily shrugged. "I don't know. Think of something!" She disappeared into the shadows at the back of the room. James looked to The Painter, who blocked their only exit, still lost in his thoughts. James searched the room, desperate for a solution to present itself. He briefly considered tossing one of the blood-filled jars at their captor, but the sight of blood had the uncanny effect of making him faint. He cracked his knuckles. He'd have to do it the *old fashioned way.*

He flared his nostrils like an enraged bull. The Painter looked at the berserk boy before him with a mix of confusion and amusement. James rolled up his sleeves and snarled. "Prepare to feel the pain! My body is so weaponized it requires a government permit!" With another nose flare for good measure, he charged. Arms flailing overhead, he cranked his neck and unleashed a savage, Aztec-warrior battle cry.

"Ahhhhhhhhhwoooooooooooogaaaaaa!"

The Painter's eyes widened as the flapping limbs bore down on him. The delayed reaction was the only window of opportunity James needed. Scratching the air like a wild animal, he pounced.

James soared through the air with the exquisite grace of an East-African gazelle. Time seemed to slow as he glided horizontally across the room. Unfortunately, time did not seem to have slowed for The Painter. The old man took a single step to the side, allowing James to continue his elegant glide right past him.

BANG!

The magnificent flight came to an abrupt end as face met wall. James staggered back to his feet. "Is got all you that?" He shook head. "I mean...*is that all you got?*" He stumbled forward, disoriented by the way the room was now spinning like a broken carousel. As he frisked himself for fractured bones, his fingers brushed against a bump in his pocket—*the pepper spray!*

Only when James' vision finally stopped spinning did he realize that The Painter was marching forward holding a sharpened paintbrush. James guessed the raging psychopath was planning more than "face paint" with it.

James stood his ground—albeit, a bit wobbly—and waited for the opportune moment to strike. Moments such as these were what marked the worth of a man. Such occasions separated the men from the boys and the lions from the mice. This was the landmark showdown that his children's children's children would one day speak about with awe and reverence, recounting that fateful night when their great grandpa had stood down a hardened killer and saved the world with nothing but his bare hands and a $1 no-name brand of pepper spray.

His hand drifted to his pocket, fingers twitching.

It was almost time.

The Painter raised his weapon.

Now!

James' hand moved in a blur of motion. He whipped out the pepper spray like an expert gunslinger, took aim for The Painter's face, and squeezed the trigger with all his might. An explosion of pepper spray burst from the can—in the wrong direction.

James experienced the sensation of bobbing for chili-peppers marinated with hot sauce in a barrel of boiling lava during the middle of a Sahara summer.

"AHHHHHHHHHHHH!"

With eyes ablaze, James had no idea how close The Painter or, more importantly, his *spearlike paintbrush* were. Had he bought Emily enough time? James forced one smoldering eye open—and saw the blurry shape of a sharpened object plunging toward his heart. The point of the paintbrush reached James' chest—and then the room exploded in a blinding white flash.

The dark, cramped room vanished into an ocean of whiteness, the shelves and jars dissolving like an ice sculpture under a heat-lamp. Even James, still rubbing his bloodshot eyes, melted into a whirling rainbow of colors. The colored dust puffed away as The Painter's weapon speared harmlessly through it.

The Painter glanced around with a puzzled expression, and found Emily holding onto his arm. "What have you done?"

Emily flashed a toothy grin. "Let's just say *two* can play your game."

Anger consumed The Painter's angular face. "You little brat! You've tricked me! You've pulled me inside of a painting! *How?* The Painting Portal is *mine*! How have you done this?"

Color appeared at their feet, swirling around them like a thousand dancing fairies. With a bright flash, the colors shot out in an explosion, dyeing the white expanse. The Painter looked frantically around as the landscape began to take shape.

Emily smiled. "While you were distracted I used your extra supplies to paint a replica of this room." She tapped her nose, which was still bleeding from her fall down the trapdoor. "What can I say, you've taught me all I know! I was able to grab you right before you killed poor James. I suppose I owe you a thank you. It was *you,* after all, who told me how to bring another person into a painting portal." She scratched her head. "Or at least the *other you* did. This is all so confusing. Anyways, farewell!"

The Painter looked down in horror. He was now standing atop a snowcapped mountain. All around him, as far as he could see, was an endless mountain rage. "You can't do this to me!" he shouted.

"Oh, but I must," Emily said, mocking his earlier words. "Besides, you should consider yourself lucky. Not many people can say they've stood on the peak of Mt. Everest." Emily clapped her hands and a thick winter coat materialized on him. "Stay warm!"

A moment later Emily was staring at a small painted canvas. The texture was perfect, the perspective impressive. She was particularly pleased with the artwork's main attraction—The Painter's face was as white as the snow around him. *All in all, not bad,* she thought.

Sprawled on the ground at her feet, James was still trying to clean the pepper spray from his eyes. He glanced up with puffy eyes. "All I can see are red splotches. Am I dead, or did we win?"

Emily smiled, reaching out a hand to help him up. "We won. He's gone. Or at least one of him is. I must admit, you were an effective distraction, although rather...how shall I put this...*unorthodox.*" There was no time for a victory celebration. "We've got to stop the other Painter before Ricky finishes that masterpiece."

They dashed from the room, hoping Van Gogh was not lurking nearby. When they emerged from the room they found the coast clear. Light flickered from the open door at the other end of the hallway. "Quick!"

The sound of their footsteps echoed down the corridor as they sprinted toward the light. Neither dared dwell on the consequences should they fail. James kicked the door open and they burst into the room.

The Painter and Ricky had their backs to them. At the sound of the opening door, they both turned. Ricky shook his head slowly. "I'm sorry, guys."

He stepped aside, allowing a clear sightline to the canvas.

Emily cupped her mouth.

The painting was finished.

They were too late.

Second Chances

Ricky didn't know how to act after having just doomed the entire human race. In fact, he wasn't entirely sure *how* he had doomed humanity, only that a queasy feeling in his gut told him he had. He briefly wondered if his mother had experienced similar symptoms after giving birth to Catherine....

Catherine!

His little sister's face appeared in his mind. If he failed to stop The Painter tonight he would never see her again. Who else would he torment? No. He would *not* fail. If nothing else, he would go down swinging.

"At long last, I have succeeded!" The Painter bellowed. He grabbed the tarp that concealed the painting. "Behold, my masterpiece!" With a *whoosh* he yanked the cover away, revealing the full painting beneath. Ricky's heart fell. At least now he knew *how* he had doomed the world: he had turned The Painter—a murdering lunatic—into God.

They waited in anticipation. Ricky scratched his forehead. *Anticipation for what?* The masterpiece was finished. Didn't that mean the dreadful deed was already committed? Every other time the impact of the painting portal was immediate, becoming reality the moment he returned. Did that mean The Painter was now God? Ricky had always imagined God would look, well, *different*. More like Santa Claus and less like the creepy old man before them.

The Painter appeared to arrive at the same conclusion. "I don't *feel* any different." He glanced back to the finished painting. "I don't understand. Why didn't it work? It *should* have worked. I did everything right!"

"No, you didn't." Emily stepped forward. "The *other you* told us that the reason you can't paint yourself as a younger man is because you no longer remember who that man was. That version of yourself has been crushed into oblivion by heartbreak and pride."

The Painter scowled. "And what does a silly little girl like you know of such matters?"

Emily glanced at Ricky. "Just this week I've seen pride steal away my best friend. I've felt the sharp pain of jealousy. I've experienced bitterness that caused me to lose sight of what really matters in life." She inhaled a deep breath. "You can't paint yourself as God because you don't comprehend God. You see him only as a rival. Your *masterpiece* is just a bad imitation of Michelangelo's vision."

"Perhaps," The Painter snarled. "But in my genius I anticipated such a problem." He stabbed a boney finger toward Ricky. "That is why I used *him*. I knew he'd be easy to manipulate, yet he still possessed enough childish innocence to see hope in this cruel and evil world. So, little miss-know-it-all, explain why *he* couldn't make the painting work either!"

Ricky scratched his chin. The man, raving mad as he was, had a decent point. Emily didn't hesitate. "*You* of all people should know the answer to that question. You've forgotten one of the most basic foundations of art."

The Painter leaned forward, expectantly. So did Ricky and James. Emily let the silence linger for a moment, before answering. "Intent."

"Huh?"

"Intent," Emily repeated. "The reason why an artist paints a particular work. Nothing ruins art quicker than an artist without conviction. An artist who doesn't truly *believe* in what they are painting can never achieve greatness." She motioned toward Ricky. "You can teach someone *how* to paint; you can tell them *what* to paint; but you can't convince them *why* to paint. *That* is why you have failed, Mr. Fredrick

Flaymore."

The Painter's face contorted at the sound of his true name. "It seems *you* have forgotten a vital part of art as well. *Perseverance*!" The words dripped from his mouth like venom. "Having already achieved immortality, I have plenty of time for second chances. I *will* complete my masterpiece, one way or another." He reached to his table and retrieved a large paintbrush. The brush's handle was whittled into a sharp point. "Unfortunately for you three, I cannot allow you to interfere with my plans any longer." He stepped toward them. "Which is why I have to kill you."

Death By Paintbrush

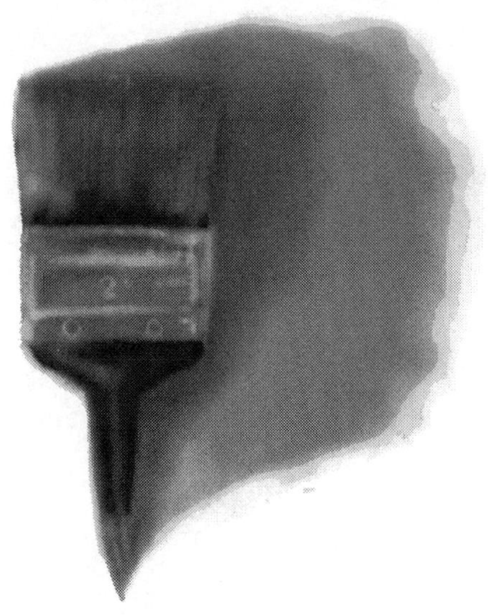

Ricky had never spent much time envisioning his death. If he *had,* he was reasonably sure he wouldn't have wagered on *death-by-paintbrush.* He supposed there were worse ways to go, although at the moment he couldn't think of any. The

Painter began to pace toward them, murder in his eyes. Ricky's pondering was cut short by James, who pulled him and Emily into a huddle.

"We have approximately sixteen seconds to come up with a brilliant plan or else we all die." Ricky looked into James' determined eyes, or at least he *assumed* they would look determined were they not bright red and swelled to the size of golfballs.

"What in the world happened to *you?*"

Emily slapped his arm. "Fourteen seconds."

Ricky scanned the room

"Twelve seconds...."

"The countdown's not helping, Emily!" James said.

Ricky's eyes lit up as he spotted something. He had a plan. A terrible, desperate, long-shot plan, but beggars couldn't be choosers. "Okay, listen up..."

Emily immediately shook her head. "That won't work. I can't do it."

"It *has* to work. I have faith in you Emily."

"That's not how you felt the other day when you thought my portrait of you was a hideous *monster*!"

"Three seconds," James squeaked, picking up the countdown.

Emily groaned, but nodded. "Fine. I'll do my best."

"Good, because we're out of time. *DUCK!*"

They dropped to the floor just as The Painter's weapon whizzed through the air above their heads.

Ricky grabbed James. "This way!" They staggered to their feet as The Painter readied for another attack. With a quick nod to the others, Emily rushed off in the other direction. Ricky hoped it wasn't the last time he'd ever see her. Now it was time for James and him to do what *they* had to do—first and foremost of which was *to not die*.

Ricky wasn't sure their idea would work. But even a dismal 1-in-10 chance of success made it their best option by a country mile. He ran straight toward The Painter's failed masterpiece. Reaching the canvas, he scooped up a paintbrush and coated the bristles with fresh gob of the blood-and-jasmine scented paint.

"Noooo!" The Painter roared. Ricky grabbed James' arm and pressed the brush to the canvas. The room spun as they were both pulled into the painting portal.

Emily scrounged through a pile of The Painter's possessions, periodically glancing over her shoulder. Despite having seen the scene before, the sight of Ricky, James, and The Painter standing still as statues in front of the canvas was no less bizarre. They appeared no more alive than the inhabitants of a wax museum. That is, except for the indiscernible blur of motion from Ricky and The Painter's paintbrushes as they attacked the canvas like two dueling swordsmen.

A rainbow of colors danced in elegant swirls across the canvas' surface like a retro computer screensaver. Emily knew that whatever was taking place inside the painting portal was far less lovely. She stood, arms full, and returned to the room's center. In doing so, she caught sight of movement out the back window—a large shape prowling through the foggy graveyard.

Despite having never seen the beast before, there was no mistaking its identity: Van Gogh—and *not* the cute puppy version. The creature's head lifted, its ears perking up like a startled deer. Then, as if drawn by some devilish telepathy, the monster turned and looked directly at her.

Emily froze. There was no use hiding. She had already been spotted. The stare-down lasted for several more excruciating seconds. Then the grotesque pet raised onto its hind legs and released a shrilling howl into the moonlit night. Dropping back onto its front feet with a resounding *boom,* the monster galloped toward the house. There was no doubt in Emily's mind where it was heading—it was coming for her. She glanced at the bundle in her arms. There wasn't much time.

The first sight Ricky saw upon entering into the portal was The Painter. His deranged face had the look of a man with an unquenchable hankering for murder. Ricky yelped. The alarmed cry was echoed by James in a pitch usually reserved for dogs.

The Painter stalked toward them. Ricky snatched James by the sleeve and fled, soaring above the cloudy landscape that stretched all around them. The Painter gave chase.

Ricky had *expected* the madman to follow them into the painting portal. In fact, he had *hoped* The Painter would follow. He and James needed to keep him busy until Emily finished her part of the plan. What he had *not* anticipated was that The Painter would be already waiting for them. *How was that even possible?* Ricky instantly realized the answer. *Because he was already here.*

Ricky halted, twisting around to see The Painter's arms lashing out for his neck, mouth wide and teeth exposed as if he planned to bite his head off. Ricky threw his arms up to brace himself and blinked. The Painter's body detonated into a puff of colored mist. The streams of color washed over Ricky like water vapor, dyeing his skin with rainbow pigments.

"You did it!" James exclaimed. "You defeated The

Painter!"

"No," Ricky said. "That wasn't him. Not the *real* him, anyway. That was only the version I painted of him."

James scowled. "If that wasn't the real Painter, then where is he?"

"Right behind you," said a raspy voice.

A hand grasped James' mouth, silencing his scream. Ricky spun to see The Painter grinning with unhinged amusement. James was held captive under one of the murderer's arms, the sharpened tip of the paintbrush pressed against his neck.

"A brave *but foolish* decision to enter into my own masterpiece," The Painter gloated.

"It's my painting, too," Ricky said. "You said yourself that collaboration is a part of the artistic process. I have as much control here as you do."

The Painter chuckled. "I also said collaboration was *highly* overrated. The problem with partners is that one is always more talented than the other. The stronger is always pulled down by the weaker link."

Ricky shrugged, conceding the point. Many of his school peers during assigned group projects had told him the same. The Painter motioned to their surroundings. "This is *my* world. *I* am the stronger. I may not yet rival God, but in *this* world I have no equal...*least of all* the likes of you!"

Ricky puffed his chest out in defiance. "We shall see about that."

"Indeed, we shall."

Ricky cracked his knuckles. "May the craziest imagination win."

The Painter sneered. "And the weaker partner *die*."

The scene erupted in a blast of color.

Battle of the Imagination - Part 1

Sweat zig-zagged down Emily's forehead, rolled over her chin, and dripped onto the canvas below. "Blast!" She quickly dried the splotch with her sleeve. More nervous sweat continued to drain down her flushed face. *Pull yourself together, girl!* An eerie moaning sound resounded behind her.

She craned her neck, but there was still no trace of the monster. Emily knew full-well that eventually she would look back and find the colossal beast filling the door frame. For painfully obvious reasons, it was imperative that she finish her task before that happened.

Ricky's plan was simple. While he and James kept The Painter occupied, she would use blood-paint to paint a reconstruction of that fateful moment in Mumzy's teashop when he had stabbed a paintbrush through his heart. If successful, it would change the outcome of that catastrophic day and prevent The Painter from ever discovering the painting portal. Or, at least they hoped it would. The list of things that could go wrong was as lengthy as the backlog of detentions Ricky owed Mrs. Martin for "lost" homework.

The task itself shouldn't be too difficult. Creating a painting from inside the portal was easy. Plus, this time she had a picture for reference! She reached into her pocket to retrieve Mumzy's photograph—and found nothing. Frantically frisking her other pockets, she found nothing but a lint-covered nickel and a wad of old candy wrappers. *Double blast! I must have dropped it in the other room.*

She *needed* that picture. Without the image for reference, she was lost. She rushed to the door to retrieve it, but froze in the entranceway. The awful moment had come at last. Standing at the far end of the hall, its immense body filling up the entire passage, was Van Gogh. The hungry creature released a spine-chilling howl—and charged.

Ricky was hurled through the air as the thick clouds around him churned, forming into a dozen violent twisters. All sense of direction was lost as he was whirled around and around and around and around and around. As he cartwheeled out of control through the sky, he swung his hands at the tornado to blotch it out as he had done to the fake Painter.

Nothing happened.

Ricky waved again with increased gusto.

Nothing happened.

Only then did he remember The Painter saying that he would be able to *interact with* but not *change* Ricky's creations. The same must be true in reverse. There was no limit to what they could each create with their imaginations, but they were powerless to erase what the other had conjured. If Ricky were going to win, he would have to use his substantial wits. *Bring it on, you tea-loving creep!*

Color spewed out from beneath his feet. A moment later a heavy, rusted chain was fastened to his leg. Connected to the other end of the chain was an enormous freight ship. The 100,000-ton boat plummeted downward, towing Ricky along for the ride.

As he concentrated, a vast blue ocean materialized below him. A massive tidal-wave splashed up as the barge crashed into the water. As Ricky careened toward the ship, he clapped his hands and the ship's cargo instantly morphed into a mountainous, fifty-foot high mound of feathers. The downy heap cushioned his fall, launching feathers like New Year's confetti into the air.

"AH-CHOO!"

The sneeze sent even more feathers fluttering in all directions. Ricky had been too busy trying to avoid becoming a blood-and-guts pancake to remember his allergies. With a snap of his fingers, the feathers turned into water droplets.

Ricky shook a fist at the gray storm clouds above him and bellowed, "Is that all you've got?"

The Painter appeared through the clouds, floating like a graceful snowflake. James was still trapped in the murderer's tight grip, his face green from motion sickness. James was terrified of flying in *airplanes*. Soaring through the air superman-style was undoubtedly a most unpleasant experience. The Painter landed softly on the deck. "Be careful what you wish for, foolish boy."

Crash!

Ricky flinched at the thunderous sound.

What on earth was that?

Crash! Crash! CRASH!

He looked up and received his answer.

It was raining...cannonballs.

The iron spheres burst through the ship's deck. A shadow appeared around Ricky, growing bigger and bigger. He dove aside as a cannonball splintered the wood where he had just been standing.

I'm going to get pulverized!

He dashed across the deck with his hands overhead, dodging the incoming cannonballs and avoiding the holes. He reached the ship's railing and dove right over it. His arms extended into an arrow's point as he torpedoed toward the water.

Smack!

A hard belly flop reminded Ricky why he had never been able to pass red-badge in childhood swimming lessons. Doggy-paddling in place, he watched the ship sink beneath the water. *Where'd The Painter go?*

Something brushed against his leg. He turned, expecting to see his nemesis. What he saw instead was the world's most gargantuan shark fin. *This just keeps getting better and better*. The great white shark circled him, eyeing him up like a floating buffet. It completed its third loop—then launched forward.

Ricky slapped the water, causing it to lift in a gigantic wave, carrying both him and the ravenous shark along for the ride. Ricky rode atop the thirty-foot wave like an expert surfer. He watched in disbelief as the monstrous fish swam *up* the wave toward him. *And I thought* Catherine's *appetite was scary!* The shark's gaping jaws opened to devour him.

Ricky jumped from the top of the wave—and continued to fly, powered by a newly created jet-pack. He scanned the sea, searching for James and The Painter. The water below started to bubble. Then, like a floatation device pulled to the bottom of a pool and then released, an entire mountain burst up from beneath the tide. Ricky hovered toward the new landmass, certain he'd find The Painter there.

His assumption proved correct. The Painter stood in the center of the island with his arms extended in open challenge. Beside him James was trapped in a giant birdcage. Ricky did a double-take. *Either James had gotten shorter or else....*

He realized the cage was sitting in the middle of a large patch of sinking sand. The sand was already up to James' chest and rising higher by the second. Before Ricky could attempt a rescue, a booming sound stopped him cold. He had watched *Jurassic Park* enough times to identify the unmistakable roar of a Tyrannosaurus Rex. He groaned. "Emily, *any time* now!"

Battle of the Imagination - Part 2

BOOM!

The door rattled, threatening to burst off its hinges at any moment. Emily didn't bother looking. If the monster broke through the lock, the razor sharp fangs in her back would let her know. She fixed all her attention on the canvas in front of her. Her entrapment in the room presented two grave complications.

First, she now had to replicate the photograph *without the photograph* for reference. Thus far she had gotten through thirteen years of life religiously avoiding three things: wearing socks with sandals, eating 99-cent gas station chili-cheese hotdogs with relish, and painting without a reference picture. Now she was forced to break the most serious of those life rules. Doing so also meant facing her arch nemesis—*a portrait.*

The second equally dire complication was that the rabid beast on the other side of the door also separated her from The Painter's storage of tea-leaves to add pigment to her blood, as she had done earlier. As a result, she couldn't use her own blood to enter the painting portal. She remembered overhearing The Painter say that he had spilled paint on the image of Ricky's lost shirt, and the painting had still come true. That must mean the transforming power of blood-painting worked even if you didn't enter the portal. At least she *hoped* that's what it meant.

Emily rolled up her sleeves. She'd have to do things the *old school* way—by hand. Without the advantage of creating from inside the portal, her painting would have to be absolutely *perfect* if this was going to work.

There was still no solution, however, for her lack of magical paint. An idea suddenly lit up in her mind. It was her only chance. She dipped her brush into The Painter's leftover blood-paint. She had no idea whatsoever if using another artist's blood worked the same as using your own. She added a drop of her own blood from her bleeding nose for good measure. *Would it be enough?* Would it still have the power to change the world? She *was* sure that being eaten alive by a monster gave her a *zero percent* chance of success, so anything else was worth a try.

She examined the features of The Painter's face, who still stood petrified beside Ricky and James. The swirling color on his masterpiece continued to change like a disco ball. The color raced across the canvas like hundreds of shooting stars, exploding into a bright medley of shapes and objects.

Wait, was that a dinosaur!?

She forced herself to look away. *Concentrate, girl!* She pressed her brush against her own canvas and began to outline The Painter's silhouette.

BOOM!

The door rattled again as the monster rammed against it. Emily hoped Ricky and James were faring better than she was. Although, knowing Ricky and James, she had serious doubts.

Ricky ran for his life, screeching at the top of his lungs like a tween girl at a boyband concert. The entire island quaked as the T-Rex gave chase. Ricky inwardly kicked himself for not having thought of dinosaurs first. *That should be off-limits!* The ancient predator bellowed another savage roar.

Ricky snapped his fingers and a walking stick grew in his hands. Seconds later the massive creature burst from the trees and began tromping down the beach toward him.

Ricky waited anxiously.

The T-Rex was almost within striking distance.

"Hey, pea-brain. Don't you know you're supposed to be extinct? I'm going to kick your butt all the way back to the Jurassic age!" Raising the stick above his head, Ricky traced a line from the sky down to the beast. The T-Rex opened its jaws, revealing its enormous teeth.

A faint hum buzzed in Ricky's ear, starting soft and growing louder. As the T-Rex lunged to gobble him up, a bright ball of light flashed across the sky. The dinosaur's final roar was silenced as a fiery meteor crashed into it.

When the dust settled, only a deep crater existed where the dinosaur had been. *I just beat a T-Rex,* Ricky realized. The longer he thought about it the more impressed with himself he became. *That's unquestionably the most manly feat ever done in the long history of manly men.*

He rushed back across the beach and found The Painter still waiting. The quicksand had swallowed more of the birdcage and now reached James' chin. Seeing his brother, James yelled. "Don't just stand there, *DO* something!"

"*Do* something? I just beat a freaking *T-REX!*" Ricky sighed. *I never get any credit.* He faced The Painter. "Let him go! It's not too late. You're not a bad man. You're just a normal guy with a slightly insane, diabolical desire for ultimate power and world domination." Ricky scratched head. "Okay, maybe you *are* a bad man."

"Eloquently said, Shakespeare," James mocked. "And you say *my* speeches are bad. At least I *ahhhh...*" He was cut off mid-sentence as the sand rose above his mouth.

"Can't you see? I've already won!" The Painter laughed. "How about some fireworks to celebrate my victory?" He danced his hands through the air like an orchestra conductor.

Boom!

The mountain peak exploded as a bright scarlet substance shot into the air. Ricky realized that the *mountain* was, in fact, an *active volcano*. The lava came roaring down the slope toward the beach.

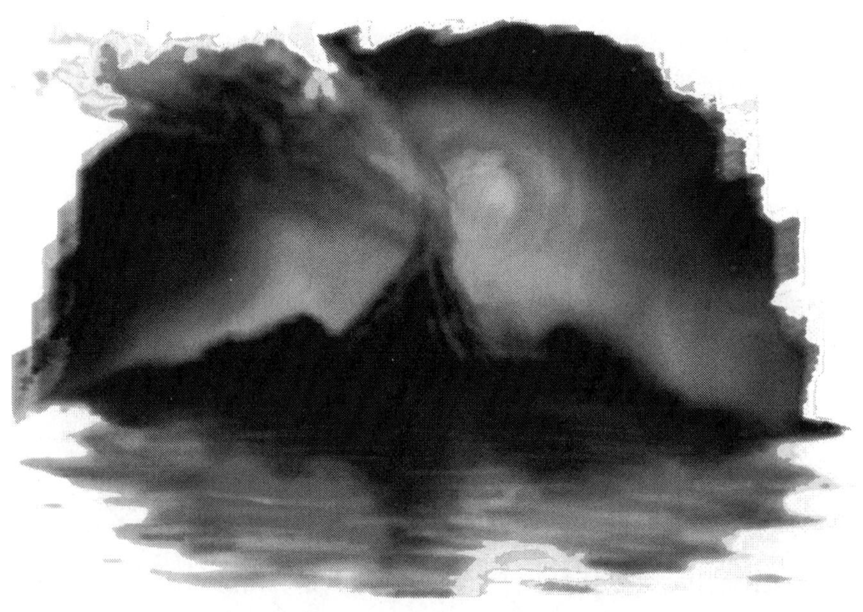

Ricky trudged through the sinking sand to where only a tuft of James' hair remained visible above the surface. Grabbing the top of the birdcage, Ricky heaved with all his might. The cage didn't budge. He tried again. It still didn't move, and this time, neither did his arms. In dismay he realized that *he* was now trapped by the sand as well.

Think! Think! Think! The intense heat wave and the popping sound of the bubbling lava made his mind foggy. All the while he continued to sink deeper and deeper into the pit. He supposed he should have done the thinking *before* running like a wild man into the sinking sand.

"Farewell, my friends." The Painter bowed and then vanished, his body fizzling away into thin air.

He's left the painting, Ricky realized. *He's going back to get Emily!* Ricky looked toward the volcano, sweat pouring down his face as the scalding lava oozed toward them.

Emily flinched as the door exploded off its hinges. The musky stench of wet fur permeated the room. She jumped to her feet and spun around. The massive creature stood in the doorframe, its long tongue sliding back and forth across its black lips.

A voice sounded from the other side of the room, "Oh, I

do hope I'm not interrupting anything. Intruding during dinner time is *extremely rude*, after all." Emily's eyes darted to The Painter. Ricky and James stood petrified beside him. *They're still trapped in the painting.*

Her eyes danced back and forth between The Painter and his freakish pet, then looked to the painting in her hand. Everything, from the teashop to the portrait of The Painter, had been completed to the best of her ability. Only one tiny background detail remained unfinished.

Alarm flared on The Painter's face as he recognized her painting. He and Van Gogh both started forward, but they wouldn't reach her in time. With satisfied grin, Emily whisked her brush down and completed the final detail. Panting for breath, she raised her finished work victoriously into the air. After a moment her smile faltered. The painting was finished and nothing had changed.

The plan had failed.

"An interesting try," The Painter said, taking another step toward her. "Unfortunately, it appears you lack the talent to achieve the greatness you desire." Emily continued to gaze at the finished painting in disbelief. *Was it because she had used The Painter's blood-paint instead of her own? Had her portrait of the Painter been too unrealistic? Why!?* Whatever the reason, she had failed. They had lost. Now they were going to die.

The Painter continued to gloat. "So pitiful to think you could out-paint *me,* the greatest artist who ever lived!" He motioned to the painting in her hands. "A master artist such as myself would be *embarrassed* to ever put my name on such rubbish."

A lightbulb flicked on in Emily's head. "That's it!" She dipped her brush back into the paint.

"What are you talking about?" A hint of concern broke on The Painter's face.

Emily smirked. "You just reminded me that I forgot to put my signature on the work! Every artist knows a painting isn't truly complete until they've signed their autograph, right?"

The Painter's face went ghost white. "Nonsense," he said, but his voice was quivering.

Emily lowered her brush to the painting. The Painter and Van Gogh both lunged to stop her. "NOOOOOOOO!"

She stroked ***E.S.*** on the bottom corner.

The sinking sand scratched the bottom of Ricky's chin. This was a substantially better fate than poor James, who was now completely submerged. Ricky felt sad for this brother. James' most dreadful nightmare was about to become true—he was going to die with un-styled hair. Ricky couldn't move an inch. All he could do was watch the smoldering lava continue its relentless advance across the beach, like a great army routing the straggling remains of an inferior opponent. The tips of his hair began to sizzle from the heat as the lava rolled closer.

Twenty feet...

Fifteen feet...

Ten feet...

Ricky wanted to turn away but couldn't.

Five feet...

Two feet...

Ricky winced.

The world exploded in a blinding burst of white light—and everything went black.

Truth is Stranger Than Fiction

Ricky massaged his blurry eyes. The world slowly spun back into focus as if he had just woken from a hundred-year slumber. He was sitting on the cold wooden floor of a large room. *Where am I?* He couldn't remember how he had come to be in the dusty room. The compartment of his brain where the memory should have been was as hollow as the two severe cavities plaguing his back molars.

James sat beside him. As usual, his older brother was utterly oblivious to the world apart from his perfectly spiked hair. Next to him was Emily. She was holding a painting and had an amused grin on her lips. The sort of smile a person makes when they've just learned a juicy secret and have absolutely zero intention of keeping that secret *secret*. Finally, filling out the circle, was Catherine.

His little sister had an agitated scowl on her face. "*Excuuuuse me,*" she droned. "I was in the middle of telling you about my field trip. Are you even listening to me?" She rolled her eyes in disgust.

Ricky looked across at the still-beaming Emily. "What's up with *you?* I haven't seen you this happy since Skippy Smith won Season Twelve of *America's Greatest Nose-Whistler*."

She squeezed her lips together, struggling to contain whatever words were so eager to burst out. Knowing Emily's inability to keep a secret, Ricky simply waited. Several seconds later, right on schedule, the words began pouring from his best friend's mouth.

"I have the *craziest* story to tell you guys!"

"I already *was* telling a story," Catherine said, clearly annoyed.

Emily chuckled. "Trust me. My story is more exciting than your tour through Gallowood's water treatment center." Catherine's face suggested she wasn't convinced, but she relented. Emily looked around the circle. "But before I tell my story, do any of you recognize this man?" She displayed the canvas in her hands. In the middle of the painting a man lay on the floor of what looked an awful lot like Mumzy's teashop. Beside him lay a beautiful rose.

James shrugged. "Sure. Everyone knows that picture."

"They do?" Emily asked.

"Of course," Catherine said. "You can't enter into Mumzy's shop without her showing the famous photograph and telling the whole story of her great-grandfather."

"The man in this painting," Emily said, pointing to the figure on the floor. "Is Mumzy's *great grandfather?*"

Ricky nodded. "Yeah. What was his name again? Frodo? No, no. Fitzgerald? No, that's not it either. Hmmm..."

"Fredrick?" Emily suggested.

"Yes! That's it. Fredrick Flaymore. The famous artist. Married to Jeanie Flaymore." Ricky paused, eyeing Emily suspiciously. "Gosh girl, we're sitting inside the Flaymore's house right now! They're both buried in the backyard, *for crying out loud*. Look!" He pointed to a large portrait hanging on the wall. A middle-aged woman with a stark resemblance to Mumzy stood next to the man from Emily's painting. Both their faces glowed with overflowing mirth.

"Has Jeanie ever told us how her great-grandparents met and were married?"

Catherine scooted forward. The only thing she loved as much as death-by-chocolate cheesecake was sappy love stories. "They were both lovers of art and beauty." She paused and gave a long, savoring sigh. "At first her father refused to give his blessing because Fredrick was too arrogant and ambitious. For a while Fredrick lived like a crazy hermit and tried to become an even greater painter. Apparently he was even jealous of *God!* Can you imagine something so ridiculous? Well, anyways, he eventually realized his mission was impossible and returned to Jeanie's tea-shop to propose."

Catherine scratched her chin. "There *is* something odd though. No one, *including Fredrick* himself, knows why he was laying on the floor of her teashop. Some people think he fainted out of nervousness or maybe from the overload of smells or something."

"No, that's not it," Emily said. "The store's final customer that day had spilled their sample cup of herbal tea. Jeanie had mopped up the mess before going to the backroom to close shop. The floor was still wet when Fredrick arrived with a rose and the intention of proposing. He slipped and fell. Jeanie, who heard the crash from the back room, rushed out and found him. And the rest, it seems, is history."

Catherine scowled. "That's a *very specific* possibility."

"It's not a possibility. It's the truth. At least, it is *now*." Emily sighed, letting her shoulders relax. "I can't believe it worked. I actually did it. I'm terrible at painting people, but I did it. I painted the perfect portrait."

Three confused faces stared back at her, each of them looking as if she had just spoken a high-dialect of deep-wood Elvish. Emily set the painting down in the middle of their circle ready to share her tale. "Better get comfortable...."

"...And then, while Ricky and James were distracting The Painter inside his masterpiece, I replicated the photograph. I had only hoped to prevent The Painter from discovering the magic painting technique. I didn't anticipate that everything would turn out so happy! The moment I finished the painting, the room exploded in a white light, and then I found myself here with you three." She took a deep breath and awaited their response.

Ricky went first. "You're crazy! That's the most bizarre story I've ever heard!"

"I agree," James said. "Do you *really* expect me to believe that I had *flat* hair?"

"Or that I didn't exist?" Catherine said.

Ricky scratched his head. "Hmmm, maybe this story isn't so..."

"Don't you *dare* finish that sentence," Catherine warned.

Ricky swallowed his words, deciding to change course. "It's a ridiculous story, but that's the reason I'm tempted to believe you. From anyone else's mouth it would be insane, but we all know that you have the imagination of..."

"A mud-covered brick?" Emily finished.

Ricky shrugged. “I was going to say *a dirt-crusted cement block*, but either one works. My point is that there is no way you could have come up with a story that crazy all by yourself. And besides...” He closed his eyes. Faint images flashed in his mind like an old dream he’d long forgotten. “Hearing the story was almost like *déjà vu.*”

His two siblings slowly nodded their agreement. Catherine leaned forward. “One part I still don’t understand is how the paintings had the power to change the world. What was The Painter’s secret?”

Emily laughed. “Oh, that’s easy. He just...” she paused. Her tongue wiggled eagerly in her mouth but no words came out. She frowned. “I can’t remember. That’s so weird.”

“How can you *not remember* something you just did?”

“I don’t know.” Emily scrunched her face. “I know it worked. I know I had to finish this painting in order to stop The Painter from discovering the secret. Maybe that’s it? I changed history so that The Painter never discovered the magical painting. In fact, that would mean I’ve never actually *met* The Painter. He’s been dead for a hundred years. I can’t remember the secret because I never learned it.”

Catherine sighed. “Perhaps it’s for the best. Otherwise, Ricky would just *erase me from existence* again.” She shot her brother another venomous glare. “Although it sure would be convenient to just paint a cheesecake whenever I wanted one.”

"Which is *all the time*," Ricky muttered under his breath.

"Speaking of food," James said, his stomach growling. "Let's go say goodbye to Mumzy and head home. I'm starving!"

They walked down the cobblestone path toward the white picket fence. A bed of brightly colored flowers scented the air with a glorious fragrance. Of the many houses that lined the street, the house at the end of Hallow's Drive was, by far, the most beautiful and well-maintained. They paused as they reached the gate.

On the other side of the street was a sleek black convertible car. Along the side of the car were the letters **I.M.G.N**. In Gallowood any vehicle that was not a muddy pick-up truck stood out like Frosty the Snowman at a Hawaiian luau, so the owner was obviously an out-of-towner.

The lanky man wore a black suit and black sunglasses. Below his round nose hung a thick, droopy mustache. He looked the children up and down and then jotted something down in a notepad. Once finished, he opened the car door and slipped inside. The tires hurled pebbles into the air as the car screeched away and disappeared around the corner.

"What do you think *that* was all about?" Catherine

asked.

Ricky shrugged. "Who cares, I'm starving. Let's get home. Maybe dad has some Macaroni Surprise waiting for us!" The probability of such was exceptionally high. After all, they lived in Gallowood and nothing out of the ordinary *ever* happened in Gallowood.

Or at least, that's how it used to be.

THE END (for now)

Continue the adventure in Case #2 of the Gallowood Files

There remain many unanswered questions to the strange events detailed in this case-file. How was The Painter able to bend the very fabric of reality? And what is the identity and significance of the Droopy-Mustache Man? I suspect, although I lack evidence to substantiate my hypothesis, that these events and the mustached stranger are somehow connected. So while this particular case is solved, I suspect there is much more to the puzzle than has been revealed. I will continue to investigate the strange events taking place in Gallowood (not real name) and publish my findings in desperate hope that YOU may assist me in unraveling this mystery.

The Case of The Painter's Portal – Closed.
The Gallowood Mystery – As Yet, UNSOLVED.

– Dr. Daniel R. Blackaby, Private Inspector

About the Author

Daniel Blackaby is the award-winning author of the fantasy series *The Lost City Chronicles,* as well as several non-fiction works. He is married to Sarah, and is the father of twin boys Emerson and Logan. He knows more useless Star Wars facts than any self-respecting man should, is a staunch defender of all European heavy metal music, and has a crazy passion for the Creative Arts as a means of enriching and redeeming culture. For more information on Daniel and his writing, connect with him at the following locations:

www.danielblackaby.com
www.facebook.com/danielblackabyauthor
Twitter@DanielBlackaby

WITHDRAWN

6822781230135
Siloam Springs Public Library
205 East Jefferson Street
Siloam Springs, AR 72761

Made in the USA
San Bernardino, CA
01 February 2018